GIRL HUNTED

A gripping and addictive mystery thriller

Detective Kaitlyn Carr
Book 7

KATE GABLE

Copyright

events, or locales is entirely coincidental. The author acknowledges the trademarked status and trademark owners of various products referenced in this work of fiction, which have been used without permission. The publication/use of these trademarks is not authorized, associated with, or sponsored by the trademark owners.

Visit my website at www.kategable.com

Join my Facebook Group:
https://www.facebook.com/groups/
833851020557518

Bonus Points: Follow me on BookBub and
Goodreads!

https://www.goodreads.com/author/show/
21534224.Kate_Gable

About Kate Gable

Kate Gable loves a good mystery that is full of suspense. She grew up devouring psychological thrillers and crime novels as well as movies, tv shows and true crime.

Her favorite stories are the ones that are centered on families with lots of secrets and lies as well as many twists and turns. Her novels have elements of psychological suspense, thriller, mystery and romance.

Kate Gable lives near Palm Springs, CA with her husband, son, a dog and a cat. She has spent more than twenty years in Southern California and finds inspiration from its cities, canyons, deserts, and small mountain towns.

She graduated from University of Southern California with a Bachelor's degree in Mathematics. After pursuing graduate studies in mathematics, she switched gears and got her MA in Creative Writing and English from Western New Mexico University and her PhD in Education from Old Dominion University.

Writing has always been her passion and

obsession. Kate is also a USA Today Bestselling author of romantic suspense under another pen name.

Write her here:
Kate@kategable.com
Check out her books here:
www.kategable.com

Sign up for my newsletter:
https://www.subscribepage.com/kategableviplist

Join my Facebook Group:
https://www.facebook.com/groups/
833851020557518

Bonus Points: Follow me on BookBub and Goodreads!

https://www.bookbub.com/authors/kate-gable

https://www.goodreads.com/author/show/
21534224.Kate_Gable

amazon.com/Kate-Gable/e/B095XFCLL7
facebook.com/KateGableAuthor
bookbub.com/authors/kate-gable
instagram.com/kategablebooks
tiktok.com/@kategablebooks

Also by Kate Gable

**Detective Kaitlyn Carr Psychological
Mystery series
Girl Missing (Book 1)
Girl Lost (Book 2)
Girl Found (Book 3)
Girl Taken (Book 4)
Girl Forgotten (Book 5)
Girl Deceived (Book 6)
Girl Hunted (Book 7)
Girl Shadowed (Book 8)**

Girl Hidden (FREE Novella)

**FBI Agent Alexis Forrest Series
Forest of Silence
Forest of Shadows
Forest of Secrets**

Forest of Lies
Forest of Obsession
Forest of Regrets

Detective Charlotte Pierce Psychological
Mystery series
Last Breath
Nameless Girl
Missing Lives
Girl in the Lake

Lake of Lies (FREE Novella)

About Girl Hunted

Kaitlyn Carr's hunt for the serial killer continues as she delves deeper into the mysteries surrounding her father's death.

After receiving a letter from a retired FBI agent, Kaitlyn's world is turned upside down once again. The letter claims that her father's death was not an accident, but a murder. In order to uncover the truth, Kaitlyn and her boyfriend, FBI Agent Luke Galvinson, must help the agent solve a series of cold cases that he believes are connected to the same illusive serial killer.

As Kaitlyn investigates the cold cases, she finds herself in a secluded cabin in the woods where her life is endangered. This is the perfect place for the killer to hide their victims. Kaitlyn wonders if she is getting closer to the killer or if it's the other way around. She finds herself questioning everything, from her own investigation to the people she thought she could trust.

In this seventh installment of the series, Kaitlyn's hunt for the serial killer takes her to the Pacific Northwest, a place with a near-constant cover of clouds and rain. It's a place where the beauty of nature is juxtaposed with the darkness of the killer's deeds. Kaitlyn finds herself facing a killer who is always one step ahead of her and who seems to know her every move.

With twists and turns at every corner, Gone Forever will keep you on the edge of your seat until the very end. It's the perfect addition to the Girl Missing series and a must-read for fans of James Patterson, AJ Rivers and Karin Slaughter.

Join Kaitlyn Carr on her quest for justice and the truth about her father's death. Get your copy of Gone Forever now and find out what happens in this heart-pounding thriller.

Prologue

He couldn't remember what drew him to the cabin, except that it looked warm, a glow of light standing in stark contrast with the wet, cold forest.

His nose was filled with the scent of dew on the long pine needles and the feathery ferns. It infused everything with the soft, verdant smell of growth and life.

The boy had not yet turned six, and he did not understand why his parents fought so much, or why his older brother had hit him so hard across the face the last time that he had seen him.

All he knew was that everyone in his family was quick to anger and that he couldn't handle it.

Their rage made him cower and hide.

At first, he hid in his room, then under his bed, then in the closet, and when they got to be too much, he took his bike out and rode around in the parking lot of their apartment complex.

His mom had placed a watch around his wrist that he didn't know how to use, but he listened when she said to come back when it said six.

He looked at it now. It was 7:23. He had been trying to come back for more than two hours but he was no closer to getting home.

The pines towered around him. He thought he had been following a trail, but it led nowhere. He was lost.

The thin track of bare earth vanished, the path disappeared amongst moss and boulders and twisted, gnarled tree roots. He couldn't tell where it began and where it ended.

He turned around a couple of times, trying to get a sense of where home might be. He knew that his parents would be mad and that his dad would probably get the belt from his closet. He was scared of that more than anything else.

A part of him wanted to come back and a part of him didn't. It was so late now that he was for sure going to get hit, not just by his father but by his brother, too. His brother never missed an opportunity to make him feel worse.

The boy could no longer ride his bike; he wasn't strong enough. It had only one gear, and the trail was steep and uneven, winding over rocks, moss, and the forest floor.

How could he have gotten lost here? He had no idea. He had been in the forest before, but never this far. It was twilight when he started out, the shadows were long and only got longer until the forest was all dark, with only a few patches lit by the pale light of the moon.

The light on the front of his bike didn't work. It had been kicked out by his brother. All he had was a little bit of moon that kept peeking out from behind ragged clouds scudding overhead. It was nearly pitch black under the trees. He was walking in concentric circles, while he thought that he was moving in a straight line.

Somewhere above his head, birds chirped and sang at the top of their lungs. He paused briefly when he came upon a boulder and saw a few little rocks stacked upon it in a tower.

He counted. There were seven in total, one placed evenly in the center of the other. "Who had put them there?" he wondered. "And why?"

When he lifted the top one off the pile, he saw a light flicker in the distance.

He walked his bike a little bit down the path toward the light coming from the cabin. It came from one of the windows, bright yellow, warm and comforting. The cabin was wooden with a quaint little porch and flowers out front.

Everyone he knew lived in apartments, one bedroom or two bedrooms, usually with doors that went straight out onto the landing. They looked like motel rooms, and the only time he had seen houses was when they drove by the fancy developments on the way to school.

On television, everyone lived in houses, too. There was no such thing as an apartment, and the boy often wondered when he'd be able to see someone live like him.

He had once seen someone build a cabin just like this one in a faraway place called Alaska on a YouTube channel that his father liked to watch before he opened his first can of beer for the night.

The boy loved this time with his father the most. His speech wasn't blurred. He remembered his name. Sometimes he asked him how he was doing. Most of the time though, they just sat together and watched YouTube videos projected onto the big television screen in their living room.

The TV took up almost the entire wall and it was the only thing his father had wanted for Christmas the previous year. In order to get it, his mother woke him up at 3:00 AM to wait outside of a large department store in the cold rain on a special day called Black Friday.

There seemed to be millions of other people gathered there, all waiting for their chance to run inside. When the doors opened, a couple of people got squished and had to be taken to the hospital, or so the local news reported later that night.

The boy thought it was fun. His father, after hearing that some people were sent to the hospital, laughed with his whole gut, as if this were the most hilarious thing that he had ever heard.

The boy approached the cabin carefully. He had never seen flowers in pots on someone's porch, and he wondered what kind of people lived here. He peeked in through the window and saw a shadow of someone standing in the kitchen. A woman even younger than his mother. At the long dining room table sat a man who was older, who could have been his grandfather.

The boy's stomach rumbled. He knew that his parents wouldn't give him dinner if he came home so late. He was lost, but he knew they were somewhere nearby. He just needed someone's help to find them.

He watched as the woman carried a large pot over to the dining room table and poured the man a bowl of soup using a ladle to scoop the contents of the pot.

He couldn't really see the soup, but he could imagine how it smelled and his mouth watered because he hadn't eaten since the morning. He was supposed to have lunch at school, but Trevor

Norman had taken it and told him that he would squeeze his throat until he couldn't breathe if he told anyone. He didn't, but now his stomach rumbled even more as he saw the bread being put in front of the man.

He watched as the man grabbed onto both sides of the loaf and broke it apart until the steam came out from the middle.

The boy had leaned so close to the window that he pressed his nose against it, the tip of it making an indentation against the glass.

He had no idea who these people were. He didn't really want to talk to them. All he wanted was to take some food and run home, somehow sneaking back into bed without anyone noticing. Even though he was not even six years old, he knew that this was probably not possible. No matter how much his parents drank, they always had a way of finding out. He could hardly keep anything from them at all.

He contemplated knocking on the window once again, even raising his fist to the glass, but he hesitated at the last moment. He took a few steps back without looking down. His heart jumped into his chest as he heard a loud snap. He had stepped on a branch and the cracking sound reverberated around the forest. He paused briefly not wanting to move.

What he did not know was that the branch

had been placed there on purpose. It was an improvised alarm and once someone stepped on it or anywhere around it, it would make a small dinging sound inside the cabin alerting the man that someone was outside.

The boy ran down the porch and grabbed his bike by the time the man had opened the door. He still couldn't ride it because there was no path to speak of, and the only way to get to the cabin was on foot or on an ATV.

"Hey, what do you think you're doing?" the man bellowed from the top of the porch as the boy disappeared behind a pine.

His heart was now beating out of his chest, and he could hear the blood rush in between his temples. His bike was slowing him down, but he didn't want to leave it.

The beating he would get from his father would be way worse if he lost it, but he was scared.

The man towered on the porch, illuminated and backlit by the light from the cabin.

The boy watched the man's shadow through the tree branch as he decided whether to take it with him or escape on foot.

"It's probably just an animal," a woman said somewhere inside the cabin. "You had set that up so that anyone or anything can step on it."

The boy didn't hear this part because the pounding of blood in his head was too loud.

Instead, he just grabbed onto his bike and started to roll it as quickly as possible through the pines.

The only thing he knew was that he had to get away.

Chapter 1

I shouldn't have been able to smell the scent of the rain on the sidewalk with my head pounding as hard as it was as I ran for my life. No one was after me. As soon as we got a little bit away from his neighborhood, I asked Luke to pull over and jumped out of the car and started to run. My legs continued to carry me way after my stomach was in stitches and now the pain is becoming unbearable.

My breaths are shallow as I try to grasp onto any little molecule of oxygen that I can and yet, I keep going.

Time slows down.

Every passing house seems to swish slower and slower past me even though my legs are moving faster.

Somewhere behind me, I can hear Luke

yelling my name and for me to stop, but the words are muffled and seem to belong to someone else.

I'm not a runner, more like an aspiring jogger. The pain continues to surge through my body, but I can't stop. I'm wearing low-heeled boots. Nothing too fancy, but not the kind you would ever want to run in for too long. I had gotten a head start, catching Luke by surprise when I hopped out of the car.

I head into the wrong direction down one of the one-way alleys, not so much to get away from *him*, but to just get away from what I had seen. At some point, my legs give out, and I fold in half breathing hard, holding onto my left side. My head is pounding, my nostrils flaring.

Yet, all I can see in front of me is that red crossbody bag peering out of the dresser with its distinctive half fabric and half chain-link strap design. It's the one thing that the son of my murder victim couldn't find.

Inside, Cora kept Anthony's baby pictures as well as a little heart shaped gold locket that he'd given her for Mother's Day. The chain had broken a little bit ago and she kept meaning to get it repaired. I wasn't able to see inside the purse and to confirm if the locket was there, but even the bag itself was the last thing I expected to see in this man's house. This man had become a retired FBI agent's obsession, and it was this man who was connected with three murder victims who had not known each other. But his relationship to those crimes was tenuous at best.

Still folded in half, I hear Luke's footsteps coming toward me, landing soft and even. He runs gracefully like a gazelle. After years of running track all throughout school and college, Luke knows how to breathe and how to propel his body forward.

When I find him standing next to me, he has barely broken a sweat. Only his shaggy dark curls are a little bit out of place. He puts one curl behind his ear, broadens his shoulders, and stands next to me.

"What was that?" he asks with repute. "What are you doing just taking off like that?"

"I don't know," I say, still trying to catch my breath.

"I just started to feel so overwhelmed, like out of control, and I couldn't deal with it."

"So, you just took off? Jumped out of a moving car?"

"It wasn't exactly moving."

"It wasn't exactly parked."

"Look, I lost it, okay? It just got to be too much."

It's almost as if he instinctively knows to give me space when I need it because he takes a few steps away, drops his arms to his sides, turning on his heels. I take a few deep breaths, stand up straight, and try to wrap my mind around what had just happened.

"I'm sorry, Luke, but I just wasn't thinking. I mean, maybe I was thinking too much at first, when I saw that bag, it was like, things started to connect but when I got back in the car, we were going to go talk about what happened. I just got so overwhelmed, so lost. You know?"

I had all of these thoughts all at once like, Could it be him? Are we making a mad mistake? Was it him the whole time? It's like, I just had to get out of the car, and then once I was outside, I just had to go.

"It's fine," he says, wrapping his arm around my shoulders and giving me a warm hug.

I try to pull away, but he holds me there. He gives me a kiss and I kiss him back. Despite how little my life makes sense, this part of it does; being with him.

There are no *what-ifs*, there is no *"Who's he talking to late at night?"* It's just out of the question. I trust him wholeheartedly. I know that he trusts me right back.

Given that this whole thing started off as sort of a one-night stand, it's highly unexpected, but nevertheless welcome. I pull away for a moment, take a look around, and see that there's an entrance to a trail leading off from the park not too far away from here.

"Come on." I grab his hand.

"Where are we going?" he asks, but allows me to lead him.

"Just on a walk, to get away from the houses, to get into nature and trees, and--"

"The rain's starting to pick up," he points out.

"I don't care. I'm already wet." I laugh and he smiles.

I walk more swiftly and it turns into something of a jog and he follows along. The little plaque at the trailhead says the trail follows five miles around the small lake. There's a wooden fence in the front, just a couple of slats, marking the edge of the trail. We walk as we make our way down toward the water. A rider on a horse walks by and gives us a nod.

We slow down, still holding hands and I stare deep into the horse's eyes, resisting the temptation to pet her face. She's a reddish-brown mare with enormous, deep, dark eyes and eyelashes that any girl would die for.

She flips them closed for a moment, almost like a wink as they walk away, and I grab Luke's hand tighter. When the rain picks up, he doesn't ask me how far we should go or mention what we have seen in that guy's house.

The possible connections and the implications

that if this bag belongs to our victim, there might have been a serial killer wandering around the Northwest for years now. These four victims are probably just scratching the surface.

The small lake, more like a pond, has a little dock for fishing up front and is surrounded entirely by towering pine trees whose needles shiver when the raindrops hit them. The trail winds around the lake, sometimes plunging close to shore. Other times, climbing away higher in between the trees.

I'm the first one to speak. I wish I could let my thoughts go elsewhere, but it's the only thing I can think about.

"What do you think the likelihood is it that that bag belongs to Cora?" I ask.

"Well, she got it at TJ Maxx, right? I'm assuming there were other bags made and sold between here and all the stores throughout both states."

"Yes. That's what I keep thinking, too. I mean, the connection is so tenuous. It's almost ridiculous, but there's no other bag there. I mean, there was nothing else that belonged to a woman, so why would he have a bag like that?"

"Maybe he has a woman in his life who doesn't live with him. Maybe it's a gift."

"That's possible."

"But maybe it's not," Luke says, raising an eyebrow.

I wish we could have gone into that house, put that purse into an evidence bag, and sent it to the lab, but no judge is going to give us a warrant for that. Not to mention that neither of us has jurisdiction here and we have to work with the local authorities.

"Cora died near Olympia. This is Portland, Oregon. You're talking about convincing a lot of different jurisdictions that this guy might be the guy. So far, the evidence that we have against him is slim. Just a family member in prison," Luke says, "who's telling us a story about a confession over a lot of alcohol while on a bender."

"When I first-- I know it's all ridiculous, really, I admit. Now I feel like we're falling into that conspiracy theory hole that Donald found himself in," I say, thinking back to the retired FBI agent who had first called me up here and got me involved in this case.

He wanted me to interview his friend, Victor, the guy who's in a white-collar prison, serving time for financial malfeasance, and who was the one who I told him about the confession.

I turn to Luke and say, "Donald had nothing to go on. He had very little evidence, which is why he asked me to help him, but now, it's even more loosely connected. I mean, I wonder if we're falling into the trap of looking for evidence where none exists, and just connecting the dots because we want them to connect. Humans as a species are obsessed with finding patterns among things that make no sense. You know all about people believing in causation when there's just correlation."

"That's what we do," he agrees. "We look for patterns to make sense of the world. A few good things happen on the eleventh of a month and suddenly, it's a lucky date. You rearrange your life to make sure you get married on the eleventh, you take flights on the eleventh, etc."

"Is that what we're doing?" I ask, holding my breath.

Luke says, "No."

I'm not so sure. I wonder if, given what we know about this potential serial killer, we're grasping at straws, or if we are, in fact, the only ones who really know the truth.

Chapter 2

We drive back to Olympia, Washington, and try to decide what to do about our flight tonight. Nothing is resolved and there are plenty of questions up in the air. It feels wrong to leave with so much unanswered. And yet, what choice do we have? Neither of us have jurisdiction here. All of the evidence we have seen is circumstantial at best.

We drive in silence for a little bit, listening to the hiss of the light rain against the windshield. We don't even have the radio on. The steady back and forth of the windshield wipers fights the drizzle in vain.

Just as we cross the state line on a gray highway, my phone rings, and the name Donald C. Clark pops up on the screen. He's the retired FBI agent who sent me the cryptic letter, bribing me to come up to the Pacific Northwest and help him with his case. His offer was that, in return, he was going to tell me what happened to my father, whom I had assumed committed suicide years ago. True to his word, Donald showed me evidence of foul play and murder.

I answer the call, happy to hear from him and ask him about his cruise. We haven't talked much since I visited his informant in prison, and he got the good news that his cancer might be going into remission. When I tell him that we have plans to leave tonight, he invites us over to his house for a chat, and that seems as good a place to go as any to try to make sense out of all of this.

The weathered, craftsman-style home stands proud under the overcast skies. The fence out front is lined with beautiful roses, lovingly cared for by his wife, Mary Lou. The last time I was here, she had told me that she did all the gardening herself and with the art studio filled with pottery in the back, I'm sure that she stays busy.

Mary Lou welcomes us with a freshly baked apple pie in that awkward time between lunch and dinner.

An extra slice should more than satisfy my grumbling stomach.

Donald is pushing seventy but has broad shoulders and looks like the type of man who has remained fit all his life. I'm surprised to find out that he had taken up weightlifting only a year ago and had been over 230 pounds for the last decade.

"I can't have pies like this all the time like I used to. As a result, she's not making them as much."

"Well, I certainly can't eat this whole thing myself," Mary Lou says, taking a generous bite and savoring every last bit.

We make small talk before getting down to what we're really here to talk about.

All of us seem a little bit uncomfortable at bringing it up at first because the last time I was there to discuss the case, it didn't go so well. Donald had been searching for this serial killer for quite some time, but none of the law enforcement agencies offered any support. Captain Carville flat out told me that Donald was wrong and has no idea what he is talking about and I shouldn't entertain a single thing he says. Carville talked about him as if he were simply the town weirdo; someone who should just be mildly appeased, but never taken seriously.

Donald had done everything in his power to try to get me to talk to his informant in prison, Victor McFadden. When I finally agreed, I had no idea what to expect. I came in with a lot of skepticism and the last thing I wanted was to side with a

KATE GABLE

crazy retiree who had absolutely no proof of anything.

"I told you on the phone before," I turn to Donald, taking a sip of my tea, "about my conversation with Victor. I can see why you believe him."

"And you don't?"

"I haven't made up my mind. He's very convincing, and I have no doubt that he believes what he's saying. My question is whether David Trincia just had too much to drink and wanted to feel pompous, proud, and important and decided to confess to something that he didn't do. Or if he were actually guilty."

"Why would he do that?" Mary Lou asks.

"Well, we all know that it's a lot more common than we like to let on. Cops are very good at getting innocent people to confess to things they haven't done and there are plenty of others who come forward and tell us they've committed crimes they had nothing to do with just to feel important. You know that as much as I do, right?"

Donald nods. The sour expression on his face tells me that he's not happy with where this is going, but the truth is that he has no idea.

"Look, you did your part," Donald says, putting his fork on top of his half-eaten slice of apple pie and pushing the plate away. "I can't have any more, it's going to totally derail me."

Mary Lou smiles but appears supportive of his resolution to keep to his new healthy lifestyle.

"You didn't have to come all this way," Donald says, "to tell me exactly what you already told me on the phone. *Why* are you here?"

"Well, the thing is." I lick my lower lip, buying time, trying to figure out the best way to phrase this. "There's something else that we have stumbled upon, and I don't know what to make of it, and I want to talk to you about it."

I open my mouth to explain further, but I start hesitating. Luke saves me by stepping in to fill in the gaps. He tells him about the case, about how we found Cora's body hanging in the park when we first got here, how the police have no suspect, but the primary people they're looking at are the ex-husband and the new boyfriend.

"How is this related to anything?" Donald interrupts his detailed description, making Luke twist his mouth in irritation.

"There's a connection," I say. "You just have to wait for the story to unfold."

When Luke gets to the purse, Donald's eyes light up. He's a little bit too excited like the person who sees the tiniest thread of a connection and immediately begins weaving a tapestry. That has been my worry all along.

"Does that purse have anything to do with Cora's death at all?"

"Until we get it fingerprinted and tested at the lab, we will never know. And if I break in and pull it out and gets it tested without a warrant, it's never going to be accepted in court. It's going to get thrown out. You can see the quandary, of course," I say to Donald, hoping to activate his previous experience as an FBI agent.

"All I saw was the purse and I have no knowledge of any connection between David Trincia and Cora Leonelle. All the stuff occurred in different states. The purse, while a little unique in how it looked, was bought at TJ Maxx, and I'm assuming they sold more than one of them. That's what we have so far."

"But what did you think when you saw it?" Donald asks, pointing his finger at me and leaning forward. "What did you *think*?"

"Look, I thought, yes, it could be him. Of course. I had a shiver run down my back, but I already had all these things in my mind. I'm biased. That's not what we want. We want the truth."

"The truth is biased," Donald says, looking away at the window and the crow pecking at nuts on the sill.

"The truth isn't biased," I correct him. "The truth is what it is. It either happened or it didn't. He either killed her or he didn't. That purse could be for anyone, his daughter, his friend, his friend's daughter. Who knows? He could have bought it at a thrift store or found it on the street. It could be completely unrelated."

"But it could also *belong* to Cora, right?" Donald says, propping his head up with his index finger and his thumb. "Isn't that true?"

I give him a nod.

"Yes, it's true."

Chapter 3

When Mary Lou excuses herself for a moment and collects our plates, Donald gets up and pours himself another glass of whiskey, offering to add more to my wine. I say no, but Luke gets a little bit more. He leads us from the dining room into his study. The walls are lined with bookshelves. There's a large desk in front of an oversized window looking into their back garden. Donald turns in his leather recliner to face the couch where we sit. After taking a few sips, I place my glass onto the coffee table weathered with scratches and marks, the kind that looks like it had lived quite a few lives before it ended up here.

"I've had this coffee table since my days at the FBI academy," Donald says. "I was thinking of getting it refinished, but then all the scratches would be gone, and it wouldn't be the same."

"Where did you go to school?" Luke asks.

"University of Virginia. I was going to go to law school there, too, but decided to join the agency instead. I wanted to serve this country, be part of something bigger than I was, and I enjoyed my job for many years. I rose through the ranks, and they always brought me out when they had complicated unsolved cases, missing kids, that kind of thing, or just whenever they needed a new pair of eyes to take a look at the evidence and check out all the angles."

I've heard bits and pieces of this before. But I'm not here for a biography.

"Donald, I want to ask you something," I say, leaning over. "I want you to be as honest as possible."

"Sure. Shoot."

"You believe in this case wholeheartedly. You believe that David Trincia is the one who's responsible for everything that has happened?"

"Not everything, just the three people that Victor had mentioned."

"That's what I mean," I say.

"I do believe that he killed those three people," he says. "Victor would have no knowledge of the locations of those murders. The only reason he looked them up is because of his uncle David."

"Yes, I know that."

I pick up my wine glass again, playing with it and examining it under the dim light.

"You had this desk since you were in college, too?" Luke asks.

"Yes, I don't use it much anymore, unfortunately."

David leans back in the recliner.

"I have a stand, and I put the laptop on it. It's easier for my back to sit in the recliner, zero-gravity position, all that. I've got to say, losing all this weight really helped a lot and my back is not aching so much, but hunching over papers, reading articles, doing research really takes a toll on your body."

"You don't have to work so hard anymore." Mary Lou comes into the room with a cheery, bright smile.

She's dressed in jeans and a button-down shirt that's rolled up on the arms. She has a friendly demeanor, easygoing, but not the kind that pushes to be your friend. I can see how they would've been a good match at cocktail parties and work events, with her breaking the tension that Donald had built up.

"I wouldn't even call it work anymore since I'm not getting paid. Just learning, researching, working this case."

"Obsessing over this case," she corrects him again with a gentle smile. She's not angry, it's more like she understands him after all these years, but is not particularly happy about it.

I ask her about their cruise, the one that they had planned to take, and she gushes about the excursions and the dinners and everything that they're going to see and do. Donald, on the other hand, withdraws.

I try to make light of the situation with a job.

"Hey, listen, you tell those people on that cruise what you're working on, they're going to get excited. You'll be the talk of the place. How often do they get to hear about a serial killer, right?"

"Ha, ha," he says sarcastically.

He and I both know that the details of this kind of thing are nothing that you can ever share with anyone, not until the case is built, not until all the evidence is lined up just so for the prosecutor to take it to trial; because the arrest warrant, that's just the beginning. The last thing you want is to let some killer go on a technicality because you didn't have your every last thing accounted for.

"Tell me your honest assessment about the purse," I say, taking my gaze away from the hardcover book spines: biographies of various US presidents and prominent figures as well as thrillers by James Patterson and Stephen King.

His expression becomes more serious. I'm starting to be able to tell the nuances in his face: when he's joking, being friendly, nodding to appease his wife, and when he is actually more concerned.

"I have no idea what it means, same as you," he says. "Until we find out what he was doing the day that she disappeared that night and whether he has an alibi, your guess is as good as mine. It is a mass-produced purse, but as far as I know, he doesn't have any women in his life. At the same time, Victor hasn't been as close to him now that he's been in prison. So, who knows? It could easily be a gift, but it could also be more than that. Now, I have a question for you."

"Uh-huh."

"You have a flight home today. Are you going to be on it?"

"I only took off these days. I'm already going to have to pay for it with a lot of overtime. We have no jurisdiction here whatsoever and to find out anything would take a long time."

"Yes, yes. That is all true," Donald says. "But I have a feeling that a part of you, even if it's a small part, is considering the alternative, staying a little bit longer, maybe talking to Carville about Cora, about that purse, about what you saw."

"He's not going to be happy." I bite the inside of my lip. "You know that. He doesn't believe you. He doesn't want to hear anything about it. If I were to tell him that we went to his house to, I don't know, look into things..."

"Well, that's the thing, you're a private person, you're allowed to go and look into things, investigate, whatever you want. You looked into a window? No one has to know it was the back window behind the gate."

"That's what you think," I say. "If I want Carville to give me actual information about anything, I'm going to have to be honest."

"Well, if that's your position, why don't you just go home?" Donald says. "Your mind seems to be made up. There's no need to dwell on it much further."

I wave my hand dismissively. I know what he's doing. He's trying to challenge me and force me to confront what I really think about things instead of what is convenient. The trouble is, it's working.

Suddenly, I'm looking at my watch and considering if I have enough time before the flight to pop in by the captain's office and find out how far off I am about this whole thing. A phone call from LA wouldn't have the same impact.

"I know that you're intrigued by this case, that it's getting to you," Donald says. "Jessica got to me. There are so many unanswered questions that'll keep you up at night. But if you can't stay, I understand. You've already spent your vacation on this case."

I give him a nod. He turns to Luke, and they reminisce a little bit about their time back in training academy, of their first cases with the FBI. I head out to the kitchen to refill my glass. I don't have much time to talk to Carville if we want to catch the flight, and Luke and I haven't even talked about me staying, since it would impact him as well. Would he stay with me? Would he go back if I stayed?

"My husband only *appears* crazy, right?" Mary Lou says in her quiet, soft voice. "He worked another case like this on his own because everyone else gave up, and he got the guy in the end. It takes a lot for him to be convinced of something. He's not just a conspiracy theorist who goes on wild goose chases."

"Yes, I'm getting that sense. Still, I have no idea whether he's making any of that up."

"Who?"

"Victor, or David for that matter."

"You won't ever know unless you stay," Mary Lou says. "Will you?"

I shrug.

"You have to stay here to find out the truth, and I guess this is all about deciding how much you want to know the truth in the first place."

Chapter 4

The flight took off without either of us. We had called and changed it indefinitely, but indefinitely is not a good time to come back to work. I call my supervisor, Captain Medvil, holding my breath in hopes that his secretary wouldn't patch me through.

"Good to hear from you," he says on the second ring, and we make small talk for a little bit, me uncertain the whole time as to how to exactly broach the subject.

"You know that I went up to the Pacific Northwest, partly to get away for a little bit and partly to deal with some family issues."

"Not concerning your sister, of course," he says, very well aware of what had happened to her.

"No, not at all, but--"

KATE GABLE

"What is it, Kaitlyn?" he asks.

He's always taken a liking to me, and over the years, we've developed a little bit of a rapport. Unlike other detectives who see him occasionally, we've worked closely on more than a few cases. I'm not exactly sure what it was that connected us in the first place, but it was early on in my career when he invited me and a few others to his house. I was the only one that showed up, made friends with his wife, and we've been close ever since.

"I got this letter," I say with a sigh. "It was from a retired FBI agent, and he asked me to work a case up here and in return he would tell me more about what really happened to my father."

It got so quiet on the other end that I heard him pause whatever he had been typing in the background. Captain Medvil is well aware of the supposed suicide.

"So, is that what you've been doing this whole time up there?"

"Yes. Haven't had time to sightsee or anything like that. Been working this case. It looks like a serial killer is lurking around and has been for years. Not that many people in the agencies here believe the FBI agent, they kind of think about him as a nut, and to be honest, I thought so as well when he first called me up and asked me to do this. I didn't want to, it sounded so far-fetched."

42

I let my voice drop.

When I had first made plans to call, I was going to say that things are running behind and I missed my flight, but then the truth just kept tumbling out, mostly because I thought that I could trust him with it.

"What about your father?" Captain asks. "Did he tell you what happened?"

"Yes, he gave me the names. I listened to the tapes. There's a recording on an unrelated case when they heard the men talking about framing him and killing him in a way that would make it look like suicide, and that's exactly what happened."

"So, why are you calling me, Kaitlyn?" the captain asks, getting right to the point.

"I need more time."

"You're going to try to find the people who might have killed your father?"

"Yes, I want to, but there's more. When I first got here, we went on a hike and found a dead body. She was murdered and strung up on display, it was pretty bad. I got involved with her family, her son asked me for help, and now it looks like she could have been another one of his victims."

"Whose?"

"The serial killer's. No nickname yet."

"Well, if he doesn't have one, you better think of one."

"Me?" I ask, surprised.

"Why not? It's kind of like getting to the top of the mountain. You're the first one to do it, you get to name it."

I smile at the corner of my lips.

"How much time do you need?" he asks.

"I don't know. Two weeks, maybe three."

"I can give you ten days max, but I want you back in a week if you can swing it. We don't have that many people working now. The people I have are already working long hours, but you've worked plenty of overtime and have a bunch of time off saved up. I think I can let you go for now."

"Okay. Thanks." I smile.

I hang up the phone and a wave of relief washes over me. I wasn't sure how this was going to go, but it was a lot better than I had allowed myself to expect. The captain and I have always gotten along, and I know that helps, but I'm also certain that I'm going to have to work more than my share of overtime in the coming months to make up for this so-called vacation.

Darkness settles in and there's a knock on the hotel room door with our food delivery. Luke is still outside talking to his supervisor, but when he returns, he doesn't have the excited look on his face to match mine.

"I have to get back," he says. "I shouldn't have

canceled my flight before calling. I don't know what I'm going to do now."

"What did you tell them?" I ask.

"I told them that I need some more time, that I had some pressing matter here, but they wouldn't hear of it. Apparently, lots of people have been calling in sick, so they're getting tired of covering and working too many hours."

I know for sure that his relationship with his boss isn't as tight-knit as mine. He never really made friends. They're more like colleagues and distant acquaintances, and when it comes to favors, those people typically don't deliver.

"We should have talked this through, made more of a plan, but it's too late now. I guess you can take the next flight out," I suggest.

But he shakes his head. "No, I'm sick of all this back and forth. I'm sick of them controlling my schedule like I'm not an adult."

"You have to go back to work, right?" I ask.

He shrugs. "Maybe, maybe not."

"This wouldn't be the right way to quit."

"I'm not talking about quitting, I'm just talking about making my own schedule, taking time off that I have when I need it."

Luke paces from side to side, getting more frustrated with each step. I knew that he had been unhappy working for the FBI. He had mentioned it a number of times, more frequently during the past few months, but now it seems to be coming to a boiling point.

"I just hate the lack of flexibility in this work schedule. It's too confining. At least, your boss is understanding."

"Well, I told him about my father and what I was doing here in the first place," I start to say.

"It doesn't matter," he interrupts. "I know they have cases to work, but maybe this job's just not for me. It's too frustrating. I'm both too annoyed and bored by it. I have a lot of time off saved up because I was planning to take a big trip, but maybe it is just as well to take it now."

"But what's going to happen now? You called your boss and you said you needed time off and now what? Did you even tell him what this is about? I mean, maybe he could be more understanding."

"Yes, I did. I told him that we got a lead on a possible serial killer, and he said it wasn't his department. He said it's not my jurisdiction and I shouldn't worry about it. That guy's a total prick. He has been ever since I've worked for him and he's probably 60% of the reason why I no longer want to work there."

"But you can't just let one guy get in the way of your whole career."

"Kaitlyn, you know what we talked about before. I went into this job not entirely certain as to what I want to do. I told you that I don't see myself doing this long term."

"I know." I give him a slight nod. "But you can't just quit like this, right? I mean, what are you going to *do*?"

"I need some fresh air."

He walks out, and I know that this is more than just about his job. He's frustrated. He wants to stay here, work this case with me. It's not that he doesn't want to be an investigator anymore. I can tell that it's in his blood. Work has been making his life hell for the last six months. He doesn't talk about it much and shuts me down when I try to bring it up, but that's what's been going on. I want to offer my help, but I don't. Sometimes he just needs some space.

Instead, I call downstairs and try to make arrangements to extend our stay at this motel. They end up being booked, which is fine as well because the room was getting a little bit dreary. I check the nearby lodging situation and end up going with a four-star hotel with a pool and gym and a nice breakfast. The pictures online show tall ceilings with a marble entryway and an elegant bar.

I know that we haven't had much of a break, which was the whole point of this trip in the first place. Maybe tonight we can have a date night. I can't talk to Captain Carville about anything until tomorrow morning, anyway. Maybe this would make up for it, for a whole week of nothing but diner food.

I book the place for one night, uncertain as to what would be the best way to go about everything. We might have to go down to Portland to stake out the house some more or maybe we'll stay here longer trying to investigate what happened to Cora and seeing if any of the evidence matches up. That all depends on Captain Carville, of course, since I have no real business being here, except as a witness, the one who found her body.

When Luke comes back, I tell him my decision about the hotel, and it seems to lighten the mood. He asks to not talk about his career, but tells me that he's planning to stay for at least a few more days. We decide to put everything on the back burner and just head to the hotel, have a nice dinner, since neither of us ate the takeout that we had ordered, and maybe even a few drinks; a real date night.

Chapter 5

The Regency is nicer even than it appeared online. The room was discounted, otherwise I wouldn't be able to afford the night. I immediately feel underdressed, like my clothes should have a designer label other than a Target brand on them. As soon as we walk onto the marble tile, a woman with high cheekbones, slicked back hair, and bright white teeth smiles and welcomes us to our room. We say no to the bellhop, carrying our bags ourselves and enter a room that overlooks the pool and a beautiful, lush park below. From this vantage point, all I see are pine trees all around. No road, no houses anywhere in sight. Luke winks at me and nods at the bar.

For a second I think that the pool is outdoors, but then I realize that it's surrounded by a glass dome and glass walls, which explains why there are kids swimming down there when it is jacket weather outside.

"Come on, let me buy you a drink at the bar," he says.

I start to rifle through my bag for the nicest clothing that I can find. I'm thankful that I remembered to bring a short black dress and a nice pair of wedges, just in case of an occasion like this. I add a pair of dangling earrings and my favorite turquoise necklace along with an over-sized belt, and the look is complete. Not exactly high fashion, but decent. I tend to my lips with a dash of red lipstick. He leans over and whispers into my ear.

"You look beautiful. Okay, one rule. No talk about work, no talk about the case. There must be more to us than what we do for a living, right?"

I tilt my head back trying to remember what that would be like, what else I could possibly think about. He nudges me in the ribs and I laugh.

"I'm good with that," I add, intertwining my fingers with his.

He leans down and gives me a kiss and I kiss him back. We could just take off our clothes and get under the covers. I have a feeling that if our lips stay on each other's much longer that's exactly what we will do. So, I pull away. He has a bit of a disappointed look on his face.

"Come on, buy me that drink," I say. "I need a break."

———

The downstairs bar smells of oak, leather, and scotch. There are people sitting in suits and expensive dresses, not gowns, but the kind you wear to work if you get paid way over six figures.

Luke gets himself an Old Fashioned and I go with an apple martini, craving something sweet and tart. We sit at the far end, closest to the pool. The children are gone now, and the splashes have settled but I watch as the water moves slightly from the filtration system. It is lit up and bright blue, enticing in every way.

"You want to jump in the pool?" I ask and give him a wink.

He laughs, tilting his head back.

I've always loved his laugh. It's a way to unplug and to change speeds, so to speak. When he laughs, his whole body moves, from his shoulders down to his stomach, to his head and even the wavy dark hair on his head seems to have a bounce to it. I watch the shadows dance across his face and the way that he smiles around the corner of his mouth.

There's a little bit of crow's feet around his

eyes, but in a very attractive way, accentuating their blueness. Up here, in only a week or so, the olive tones of his skin seem to have vanished and he looks pale now. I never expected the ever-present tan from California to be so quick to disappear.

When our drinks arrive, we talk about nothing and everything. He doesn't watch much TV, instead preferring to play video games. On the other hand, I'm an addict at heart who's always on the lookout for a new show with over five seasons that I can binge in a week. You wouldn't think that I have time, but I'll forgo sleep for a good storyline. There's always a little downtime at work where I can sneak it in, even if it means having the screen off and just listening to the dialogue.

I asked him what he would like to do if he could do anything. If he were to ask me the same thing, I'd have no answer, but he does.

"I'd like to get a sailboat," he says, looking out onto the water. "I'd like to sail down to Mexico, to the Panama Canal, the Caribbean, Mediterranean, maybe all the way around the world. Who knows?"

"Have you ever sailed before?"

"A few times. Been on those pleasure sails and rented a boat, a small twenty-foot daysailer. I don't have any real experience, not much to speak of. Took a class once where we went overnight off Santa Barbara, but you said if I wanted to do anything, not what I was qualified to do, right?"

"That's it. Anyone invited on the boat with you?" I ask.

"Yes, of course. I'm not crazy. I don't want to go alone. Seriously, I'd love for you to come and whoever else comes along."

"What do you mean?" I ask.

"You know, for our family, if we have a dog one day, maybe a cat, maybe a child."

I tilt my head. "You've really thought this out."

"Kind of, I mean, not much, a little bit."

"Are you seriously talking to me about a child, though?"

I'm not sure what to think of all this and I'm not sure if it's my place to even think about it. This is his dream. I've never been on a sailboat before and as romantic as it sounds, is it even practical? Do dreams have to be?

"Don't look so alarmed. You don't have to come." He smiles and I lean over and nudge him in the ribs.

"Thanks."

"So, you really think about things like that, don't you, about us having a family, pets?"

"Of course. It can't just be the two of us, right? You've got to have some fun, got to throw more people, animals into the mix, see what happens."

"I don't know about that." I shake my head.

He laughs. "Yes, I know, you have your hesitations. One of us should, right? Good thing that I don't."

⸻

The drinks flow, and with each one, it's easier and easier to joke and to laugh despite the circumstances under which we're here. We stick to the rule of not talking about work, and instead we talk about us, the weather, but mostly dreams for the future. I ask him what he would do if he didn't work for the FBI. He tells me that he's got a lot of hobbies that have been on the back burner for way too long: writing music, woodworking, even sailing. He wants to learn more about it, but that would require trips to the ocean that he can't exactly schedule in with work.

"So, basically, you want to be retired," I say, tilting my head.

He nods. "Who doesn't? I mean, spend your days doing what you want, maybe nothing at all. Ain't that the dream?"

"Well, I wouldn't say my dream is to do nothing. Just own my time, you know. How many years do you have until retirement?"

"Thirteen. Too many."

"And what would happen if you were to quit now?"

"I don't get a pension. I mean, that's a big part of working, the overtime as well. You know that as well as I do."

"Yes."

"Retirement with a good pension is the dream, and if you can make that happen when you're still young, that's really the best outcome. That way you have money to live on for the rest of your life, and you can really pursue whatever you want, but there is a cost."

"I can't tell you what to do," I say. "Except maybe stick it out until you have more of a plan, more savings, more than just an idea of what you would be able to do after."

"Yes, I get it," he says.

"I was actually thinking of one. Now, don't laugh."

"Okay."

"How about you write a book about that detective you're working on, and then you write another and another, and you sell hundreds of thousands of copies and we live happily ever after?"

"Oh, so your idea is that I'll support you for

the rest—" I interrupt my train of thought. "You actually think I can make money writing and that money could support not just me, but both of us?"

"Come to think of it, it doesn't sound so bad," I say, sitting back in my chair, crossing my leg from one knee to the other.

The sugar and the vodka from my third martini are going straight to my head and I like it that way. He orders himself another Old Fashioned and then leans closer to me. I can smell the bourbon on his breath, but instead of being a turn-off, it draws me to him. I lean over and give him a kiss. He kisses me back. When we pull away, he narrows his eyes, just slightly tilts his head, and lets his hair fall a little bit in his face.

"I have some more of a plan, actually," he says. "What if I took everything I knew and started a private investigation business? People pay thousands of dollars to do stakeouts for their spouses, for their divorce. I could do background checks for high-net-worth individuals. I can help solve some cold cases. There won't be any benefits or anything like that, but the hours would be my own. I heard from a few friends who do this it can be quite lucrative."

"You're going to have to put in a lot of hours, nevertheless," I say.

"Yes, but it'll be in my own business. I'll control my schedule, which honestly is one of the top things that's most getting under my skin here. Being sent on different cases, not knowing how long I'll be there. Just gets tiresome, you know. Not everyone can put up with it. Some people enjoy it. They like the routine. I don't. I'd rather just take on projects I want to take on, and nothing else."

"That sounds good," I say, looking deep into his eyes. "I mean it. I'm not just agreeing with you for the agreement's sake."

"When have you ever done that?" Luke asks, and I laugh.

"No, seriously. That's probably a feasible plan. You'll still probably give notice and all that stuff to leave on good terms."

"Yes, I will. I'm not going to quit as much as I love a good 'go to hell, I'm quitting' kind of story. That wouldn't make sense, politically speaking."

"Is that why you want to stay?" I ask. "Work this case?"

"I talked to Donald today. Ever since we met, of course you've been the primary point of contact, but when you stepped out for a little bit with Mary Lou, we had a chance to speak and I do want to work this case for him. It's intriguing, if nothing else."

"Let me get this straight." I suddenly tighten my back. "You don't want to work cases that the FBI assigns you, but you do want to work this ridiculous, probably unsolvable serial killer case with somebody who's totally outside the FBI and is not going to be friendly with them anytime soon?"

"Look, it's hard to explain. He and I made a connection. You don't work for them and say you don't know exactly all the interpersonal office politics involved. It's not always a bad job, but for the wrong person it can be tiresome. He and I talked about working there. He kind of got where I was coming from. And yes, I hate to say it, but I am intrigued by this case. I do think that there's a strong possibility that David Trincia was the one who kidnapped Cora, and he took that purse as a token. Maybe I'm reading too much into it, but I want to investigate it. You're staying here. I'm going to use my days off to stay with you. I want to work this case. Donald offered to even take me on as a private investigator."

"You mean he's actually going to pay you?" I ask.

Luke shakes his head no.

"He's not paying me. He doesn't have that much money. Plus, I'll be coming with more resources and I'm putting my whole job at jeopardy."

"Yes, yes." I wave my hand in his direction and smile. The alcohol has really gone to my head and now I'm finding almost everything he says agreeable. I can't help but smile, and he smiles along with me.

"What if we actually catch this guy? What if we actually find out that he did those murders, and who knows how many others? That's such a big deal," I say, focusing hard to not slur my words.

Suddenly the possibility of fame pops into my head. I'm not one to be drawn to that, but to be recognized by colleagues and to be interviewed by a show like *Dateline*, playing an important role in solving a whole bunch of unsolved murders would be a big deal.

"What if you kept a record of it?" Luke suggests. "Why not keep a record of what we're investigating here and maybe even think about doing a non-fiction book about the story? We don't have any jurisdiction here. We can't arrest anyone. Everything official will be done by someone else. Any credit will go to the local police or the FBI working this case. What if there were another account, one from you, me, and Donald? That's why he asked you up here."

"Yes, that's a good idea," I say. "It'll be a lot of work to write something like that. I guess I'll start by keeping notes."

"You don't even have to write them down. Record them just like you do for all the other cases. Then we'll have a lot to go on, and you can write your book."

"You have a lot of good ideas, Luke Gavinson. You know that, right?"

"I try." He gives me a coy smile. He leans away from me for a moment. I can't contain the desire to kiss him.

"Let's get out of here," he whispers into my ear and grabs me by the hand.

His hands run up and down my body as he presses me against the glass elevator. His lips are soft, but his hands are strong, and his touch is exhilarating. He lingers a little bit around my breasts and then heads down south reaching underneath my dress and cupping my butt cheeks, giving them a little squeeze.

I bury my hands in his hair. He moves mine out of the way to run his tongue along my neck. When the doors open, we stumble out and continue to kiss walking down the hallway some- what awkwardly, our legs intertwining and step- ping on each other's feet.

I'm not great in heels on a normal, sober day. I toss them off immediately when he pushes me into our room, unzipping the back of my dress. It falls to the floor. I take off his jacket, unbutton his shirt, and kneel down to kiss his chiseled abs, running my tongue over the contours of each one, unwilling to wait and to savor.

He pulls me up and presses me against the wall. With one quick motion, he jerks off my underwear, and then suddenly we are one, our bodies moving in unison. My breaths are heavy, and so are his, and it doesn't take long for either of us to be satisfied.

Afterward, we collapse onto the floor in the entryway. I catch my breath and watch the way that his chest moves up and down, and the way the stars and the lights outside twinkle through the floor-to-ceiling windows.

Some time passes before he lifts my body and carries me somewhere soft. The blankets and the mattress seem to swallow me whole, and I feel like I'm floating on a cloud. When I turn to face him, I open my mouth to say something, but instead float away and fall into a deep, restful sleep.

Chapter 6

The following morning, I stop by a well-rated donut shop that the front desk had recommended and get twelve delicious, sugar-high inducing, freshly made concoctions. Some are sprinkled with sugar, others covered with frosting, and the best ones are drizzled with chocolate syrup.

Luke and I had discussed the best way to approach the discussion with the local police and decided that buttering them up might be a good way to go.

Luke stays behind, another tactical choice. Bringing in someone from a federal agency might make them feel like they're on the back foot and being watched by the higher ups. I want to go to Captain Carville and Detective Tony Mitchell with something of an olive branch.

The department doesn't owe me anything, not

really, so if I want any more information about the case than what is available publicly, I will need to get on their good side. Perhaps it's ridiculous to think that a dozen donuts would change what they would reveal to me, but it has worked in the past. It's not called "buttering people up" for nothing.

The donuts are expensive, about five dollars a piece, but they're about the size of my head, so I guess it is somewhat reasonable. I take the car, leaving Luke still in bed, luxuriating in the one thousand thread count Egyptian cotton sheets with plans to order room service. I'm jealous, especially when the rain picks up and the coat that I'm dressed in leaves much to be desired when it comes to warmth. I keep chugging my coffee and glancing over at the donuts, my mouth salivating at the sight as the scent of sugar suffuses the inside of my rental. I let out a big sigh of relief when I finally see the station and pull into the parking lot.

Captain Carville's eyes light up as soon as he sees the box from Sherman's bakery.

"I can't believe you got us those donuts."

"I'm glad you like them!"

"I wish we could eat them every day but if we made it a habit, we'd all be four hundred pounds and have absolutely no money in our savings," he jokes and waves over the people from around his office to help themselves.

I place the box on the long white table in the

front that seems to be doing the job of a little bit of everything. It collects odd papers. It holds a potted plant. It has a few scattered notebooks as well, belonging to who knows who. I move a little bit out of the way and open the box.

I got twelve and I figured they're big enough for everyone to share.

Captain Carville takes the large eclair-looking one and bites into one side. I watch as a little bit of bright yellow filling oozes from the end, but he catches it with his tongue.

"Oh, wow. This is delicious," he says and offers me a bite.

"I actually had one on the way here. I couldn't resist," I lie and stick to my coffee.

Detective Tony Mitchell, the guy who had interviewed me when I found Cora's body in the forest, gives me a slight thank you nod and grabs half of the strawberry doughnut even though I had cut the doughnuts into quarters. He wipes his mouth with the back of his hand and then chugs the last of his coffee, crushing the cup in his hand and throwing it in the trash.

"So, to what do we owe this pleasure?" he asks, looking at me with suspicion.

"The clerk at the hotel told me this place was a favorite and that I had to try it. I was just heading over and thought I'd bring a dozen."

He widens his stance and broadens his shoulders. I've been around a lot of men like him. A lot of his communication is posturing, trying to size people up as if everything's a competition. When we first met, it was all about impressing Captain Carville and how he was handling the case and my interrogation as one of the primary witnesses. It probably doesn't have to be said, but he wasn't particularly happy about me getting involved with the case and meeting with Cora's son, Anthony, on my own.

I force a smile and tell myself to be cordial, no matter what his reaction, because he isn't going to get a rise out of me. We chitchat a little bit about the weather which seems to be common courtesy around here. Then the captain asks me about my plans.

"That's actually why I'm here. I wanted to share some news with you and wanted to get your take on it."

"About what? The Cora case?"

I give him a nod.

"Just hope it falls in line with what we already have."

Now it's my turn to be taken by surprise a little bit.

"Well, we're getting pretty close to the arrest," Captain says with a big toothy grin. "I was going to call you today, but I'm glad you stopped by."

"What are you talking about?"

"The ex-husband, he's as good as confessed to it."

"What?" I ask.

"Well, not exactly. Don't mean to get your hopes up. It's not that easy. We brought him in for another interview. He admitted to having a girl-friend. He's cheating on his current wife. He said he's been following Cora. He didn't like this rela-tionship that she had with this new guy. He drove away all her other boyfriends before."

"What do you mean drove away?" I ask.

"She has dated a few people in the past. He said he reached out to them to have a small chat and things fizzled out after that. But this guy Steven Hildebrand, he's really in love with her. He confirmed that her ex-husband had made threats, but he didn't think much of it. He knew that they had a very toxic relationship, but he didn't even mention it to Cora herself because he didn't want her to get upset."

"He didn't say anything to me."

"No, he wouldn't," Detective Mitchell inter-rupts, "but that's because you're not really working this case."

"Lay off, Mitchell," Captain Carville says. "I'm just trying to tell Kaitlyn here what's happening. We brought him in, we talked to him. He agreed to let us look at his phone. We found out that he was having a relationship with another woman."

"But what does that have to do with him killing her?"

"Nothing direct. Not exactly, but he was lying to us. We pushed him on the matter and he said that he didn't want his ex dating anyone and that he had made sure that it happened that way before. Everyone kept running. He was rather proud of this fact."

"Did he actually say that he killed her?"

"No. He stopped short of that. We're going to have another meeting with him today. No matter how much we pushed, he didn't fold, but he's the primary suspect. He's most likely the one who did it."

"But don't you see? He made threats about her boyfriends," I say, "not her."

"Oh, no. He threatened her plenty. He hit her. Their relationship was clearly abusive, physically as well as emotionally."

"But wasn't that years ago?"

"Yes. We don't have much evidence of him being abusive now. But he is clearly capable of it. That's where the confession comes in."

I hesitate. I want Mitchell and the other detectives who are lurking around to leave, but I'm not sure if asking them to do that will just cause more problems and make them more suspicious of me.

Still, I need to phrase this right. What I don't have is any real concrete proof of anything, but a hunch, and sometimes that's all you have. At the same time, I wonder if maybe I'm all wrong. Maybe Captain Carville is right. If he had made threats against other boyfriends, a fact that I did not know about, who knows what he would've done?

"Can I speak with you in private?" I finally say.

The captain grabs another quarter of a donut and offers one to me. This time I can't resist. I take a chocolate one and lose myself for a moment as the sugar hits my brain. It makes it feel like everything's going to be all right as long as I can just have more of this.

"Captain Carville, I think it's a really good idea if I'm part of this conversation," Detective Mitchell pushes.

"You will be if I notify you," Captain says, urging him out and closing the door behind him.

I let out a little sigh.

"Okay. The donuts bought you some time, but I don't have all day. Why are you here?" he asks.

He sits down in a swivel chair, puts his elbows on his desk, intertwines his fingers, and waits for me to speak. I tell him the story as it happened.

He knows about going to the prison and he wasn't too happy about that before, but I don't preface it with any sort of qualifications or explanations. I just tell him what happened when we went down to Portland to stake out David Trincia's house. He listens carefully, occasionally taking a sip of the Diet Coke on his desk.

When I finish talking, I look straight at him. He pauses for a moment, seemingly taking it all in.

"You're trying to tell me that Cora Leonelle was killed by a possible serial killer, who lives near Portland, Oregon? I mean, he does have a car and he can travel, but you don't actually know if he killed those other three people. You just have the testimony of a friend of your FBI agent who wants to tell him something to keep him coming back and visiting him in prison, right?"

"When you put it that way, it doesn't sound that compelling, but the purse was right there. As I said, he has no female relatives, no known friends, or girlfriends, or wife."

"No known or not known to you? You don't know much about him, right? Everything you know, you know from Donald Clark, who's a little bit loony tunes, don't you think? Even if we were to believe him, I'm assuming that this red, very specific-looking purse was not made for Cora herself. It was manufactured by a company who made thousands of them and sold them in TJ Maxx all throughout the Northwest, possibly the whole West Coast, if not the entire country."

"Yes. Those are all possibilities," I admit.

"Okay, and you still stand by what you said?"

"Well, I didn't know what you had on the ex-husband, but this is what we have together."

"Not much," Captain Carville snorts. "Let's just say that I have a lot more. Motive, possibly a history of stalking her, bad alibi with his current wife who is saying that he's there, but once we tell her about his other girlfriend, maybe she won't be so happy to lie for him."

"Yes. That's true. That's all true," I admit.

"I don't know what you want me to say. Kaitlyn, you look at me with those big doe eyes, and you expect me to go on a whim for you, to drop everything to search for this phantom killer when you and I both know that we need evidence. We need more than your hunch about a random purse."

"That's why I'm here. I want to find more."

"But you don't work for me. You work for the LAPD, and you should probably go home."

"Is that a request?" I ask, feeling disappointed, letting my face drop in dismay.

"It's a request for now. It may become a demand. Detective Mitchell out there is not a huge fan of yours and when he hears about this--"

"I'm not asking you to cover up for me and keep me protected from him, nothing like that. I'm just asking you to think about it. What if I'm right?"

"I don't have the resources to go on these wild goose chases, Kaitlyn. I like your dedication. I wish you worked for me instead of some of these other people who are just punching the clock, but this isn't your case. Hell, it's not even my case. It's a Portland, Oregon, case."

"Not if it's Cora. Not if it's connected."

"Well, what are the chances of that?"

Chapter 7

I wasn't sure what I was expecting, but a part of me is glad that Captain Carville told me to go to hell in the first place. The ex-husband is an interesting angle that I probably dismissed too quickly, but then again, I didn't have all the facts.

Does it make me question the purse? Of course, but where do I go from here? I talk to Luke about this on the balcony of the hotel while eating a little bit of leftovers from his breakfast. Munching on some cold eggs and fruit, I relay, to the best of my recollection, everything that happened.

"I mean, he didn't tell you that he can't pursue it."

"Of course not," I say. "I mean, he wouldn't be able to really say that. As a private citizen, I can investigate whatever I want, follow whoever I want as long as, you know, I'm not stalking him. But in terms of cooperating, he seems to be focusing on the ex-husband, which makes total sense. I mean, I just brought this to him."

"I guess we'll just have to wait and see what the ex-husband's wife says, whether her alibi changes at all," Luke says.

"Let's go on a walk," I suggest. "I always think better when I'm moving."

We leave the umbrellas in the room and head straight into the woods right behind the hotel. The trail starts just past the pool and the trees soon wrap themselves around us, all emerald in color, the dew still sitting on the long pine needles.

Somewhere in the distance I spot a little deer, a baby, perhaps. Against the green foliage, she looks at me with her big wide eyes and her fur sparks a bright orange. We watch each other from a distance, me appreciating her beauty and her probably appreciating our curiosity, then Luke steps on a twig and in two steps she disappears behind the ferns.

"This place is breathtaking like this, isn't it? Without the rain."

"Yes. Well, without all the rain, it wouldn't be this green. It's the price you pay, I guess," I add. "What do you want to do?" I ask. "You want to talk to Steven Hildebrand to confirm what the ex-husband said he was doing?"

"Not really. I think the cops have that covered. They'll get more there, and you can't interrupt an active investigation by going straight to him."

"No, our best bet is probably David himself."

———

We meet up with Donald Clark early the following morning. It's barely dawn, and I had to be convinced that we should wait this long. Donald comes out with a metal lunch box with an old *Star Wars* logo on the front, as well as a backpack. He looks like he's going to his first day of first grade, his hair's combed, eyes excited, a big wide smile on his face.

Luke, on the other hand, looks pretty wrecked. There were people talking loudly outside our door, something that I slept through, but he didn't. He is still grumbling about it this morning. There was no breakfast for us and we definitely didn't plan ahead to pack a lunch. I figured I would get some takeout or we would stop by a Starbucks on the way down. The drive is about two hours.

None of us know what this is going to entail besides the fact that it's going to be quite a slog. That's probably why Donald so smartly packed things to do. Sitting in a car for long periods of time can get tiresome and boring, but you still have to remain alert in case you see something.

Somewhere on the freeway when Donald and Luke are deep into their conversation about the Seattle Seahawks, I get a text from my sister. I don't quite believe it since I have sent her numerous texts and haven't heard a word, and this is her finally reaching out. Violet didn't even want me to come down for her fourteenth birthday. She said that she wasn't making a big deal of it. Even when I insisted, Mom told me to stay home.

I know that she needs time to adjust to what had happened, but it hurt me, nevertheless. Part of the reason for this trip to the Pacific Northwest was to get away from it all.

Still, here it is, black text in the gray bubble.

What's up?

I consider what to write back. I wonder whether she's seeing the little dots on the other end of me thinking while typing.

Nothing much. I'm going to spend a day sitting in a car, hoping a guy who committed a few murders does something interesting

It takes me a few tries to word it just so, but then I send it off hoping that this would intrigue her enough to ask more. She takes the bait.

> Aren't you supposed to be on vacation?

> Yes, it didn't work out as planned. I found a dead body, got involved. Now, the guy I think did it is not the guy that the cops here think did it. Luke and I are on our own.

I decide not to mention Donald since that would unnecessarily complicate the conversation.

> I hope one of you is right. :-)

> How are you?

I decide that I have an opening to ask about her now.

> Good. Online kind of sucks, but no more than regular school.

I remember how much she wanted to go to that private school back in LA, live with me, and pursue art, something our mom was adamantly against. I'm tempted to ask about it, but that would bring too much attention onto the before and after separation that had occurred in her life, i.e., before the kidnapping and afterward. There was this life that she had before she was taken, and then there was the life that she was forced to live afterward.

> Are you getting out at all or just staying put?

I'm trying to be as careful in my language as possible. I don't want to make her think that I'm judging her in any way, and yet I'm hoping that she can somehow get over this and live the life of a normal teenager.

> I go on walks to the library, but I don't want to go back to school. Not yet. There will be too many questions. I don't want to think about Natalie.

I swallow hard. Natalie was a new friend that she had lost. I resist the urge to ask about that.

> Oh, hey! I started painting again. You want to see?

> Of course.

An image appears. I can't tell how big it is, but it's a horse's head with layered shades of blue. Parts of it are done in pointillism with little dots and parts of it with thick brush strokes.

> It's beautiful.

> It took me all week to get it just right and I just love it.

> I love that. You need to get back to your art.

I wait for her to write something else. When she doesn't, I keep the conversation going.

> Any plans for today?

I get nothing but silence on the other end.

Did I do something wrong? I reread what I had written, what she had written and wait. The dots of her typing disappeared. She had read the message and decided to ignore me for now. I know that I have to give her space, but how much? It's so difficult to gauge.

We get to David Trincia's house and position ourselves at the back of the street just in case any of the neighbors had seen us there before. I wish we had switched cars. If we do this for more than a day or two, we absolutely will. After a bit of talk about sports and the stock market, I decide to shift the conversation to something that I'm a little bit more interested in.

"Are you sure you want to do this for a living, Luke?" I ask. "This private investigator stuff, spying on people? Not all it's cracked up to be."

He smiles. My stomach grumbles as Donald breaks out his second sandwich from the back seat.

"Don't think I eat like this all the time," he chimes in. "Just sitting in the car, I figured I'd pass the time."

Now I'm happy that I don't have any chips or pretzels to snack. I would absolutely be doing that for no other reason but to pass the time.

"I was telling Luke that I did private investigative work for a little bit when I retired and that's pretty much what it is," Donald says. "You sit outside people's houses. You see if they're cheating, you tell their husband or wife, provide proof with pictures, video if you can. I think I gained about fifteen pounds doing that. That's when Mary Lou said, 'You got to find something else to do,' since we didn't need the money."

I laugh and wish that Mary Lou was here. She would add a nice balance to this conversation, and she probably would have packed me a sandwich.

"What kind of work did you have?" I ask.

"Mainly divorces. It doesn't really matter whose fault it is, but it goes to the person's character. Plus, there were a lot of people who were already divorced hiring me to watch their spouses. New love interests. To do background checks on them, see if they're appropriate to have around their kids. That kind of thing."

Around nine o'clock, David Trincia's front door opens and he walks out. Donald identifies him. He's in his 60s with short, dark hair, a bit of a slouch. He's dressed in a suit and tie, the cheap untailored variety that makes everyone look a little bit boxy. Holding a briefcase in one hand, he tosses it into his BMW 5 series and pulls out of his driveway.

The payment for that car is probably a little bit steep for a guy on his salary, though I don't know exactly how much he makes. But I know that it's a requirement for a man in this position to keep making those sales. Luke waits for the car to pull out, I note the license plate, and he drives a little bit behind the target vehicle, letting a minivan turn in front of him. Luke has done this a lot more than I have but the song and dance aspect of following a car is pretty much the same.

The wave of excitement upon seeing him for the first time wavers and disappears as I know that he's probably just heading to work. The thing about following someone is that it's painstaking and tedious. You have to establish their routine and then you have to figure out when they deviate from it.

Sometimes they'll just see a friend and sometimes they'll go and commit a murder.

Of course, we know nothing about his pattern, and the dates and times when the three victims and Cora were killed form no pattern whatsoever.

I haven't been able to find anything suspicious

about him. He has no record, not under this name. Of course, I have no idea if he has another one. It's a possibility but he has been working for the Boyden Paper Company and has been their guy on the road for years now. Very loyal employee.

We follow him to the outskirts of Portland, really an exurb, where he pulls into an industrial park and goes into the office. Hours later, after I ran in to get some takeout from a little vegan place across the street, he's still there. The morale inside the car is dwindling. The more hours I spend here, the more I wonder whether I can afford to do this.

As many hesitations as I have about him, it is unclear. The one thing that is certain is that even with the extra leeway from my boss, I don't have many days off and if I spend them like this, I'm going to regret it.

Voicing my concerns, I can see right away that Luke agrees with me. It was one thing to come out here and track him and see him in the flesh, but it's another to come face-to-face with working a case that you're not getting paid to do and are, in fact, jeopardizing your job for.

"What has stopped you from doing this all along?" I ask Donald. "If you believe that it's him and he's the one who's responsible, then why haven't you done the stakeout yourself? You don't live here, but you're much closer than we are. Only two hours away."

"And retired," Luke points out.

"Mary Lou mostly," Donald says. "She doesn't want me out of the house from nine to five, let alone twenty-four hours a day for who knows how long. You know how it works, if you leave, who knows what you've missed?"

"But you know that it's not realistic that we keep doing this, right?" I say. "I have ten days at most here and honestly, I'm regretting spending this one here. I can do some interviews. Some other background stuff. Maybe Luke can reach out to people in the FBI that you can't and see if there's anything else, but I'm not sure about this."

"Look, I know you two have your doubts."

"You have your doubts, too," I say.

My stomach grumbles again. I know that I'm partly more frustrated and annoyed because I haven't had anything to eat in a while, but I also know that I'm telling the truth.

"If you really think it's him, you'd sit out here and you'd watch, right?"

"I am not sure if he is necessarily connected to your Cora case. That's for sure."

"The other three?"

"Not really, but the hard evidence isn't there. The only way we gather more is to do work like this."

Luke and I exchange glances.

It's probably unfair to put it all on him since we're equally interested in the case. Perhaps we can give it a few more days but I'm worried that it won't be enough to keep going, but too much to give up.

Then suddenly, David Trincia comes out of his office building. It's 3:17 in the afternoon, too early to leave work, but he rushes out to his car and speeds away from the parking lot.

8

Bree

She had been alone before, but never alone like this. Sitting in a coffee shop or looking at books on the shelves in her favorite used bookstore around the corner from her school was nothing like this before. Bree Zander always liked the idea of being alone. Whenever she would watch TV shows and movies, she'd gravitate toward the scenes that depicted loneliness. A boy sitting in the corner listening to music dressed in black. A girl who stayed home and skipped the party that everyone wanted to go to.

She liked the idea of being that kind of person. She could become the main character in her own story by making TikToks and reels of herself being lonely and misunderstood. Of course, her mother didn't make it very hard. She had expected nothing less than perfection from her daughter ever since Bree was a kid. Dance lessons started at three years old, followed by ballet every evening. Her every free moment spent dancing, performing, or competing. Never once did her mother stop to ask Bree whether she even liked to dance. She didn't.

She didn't like the music. She didn't like to be whisked away and lost in her body the way that many of her friends on the dance teams said that they felt. To them, dancing was life, but to Bree, dancing was a requirement, a prerequisite to being her mother's daughter. Her mother, Mrs. Zander, previously Ms. Washington, was a people pleaser. No matter how tired she was, if she saw someone looking at her, she stood up straight and smiled. Her relationship with her husband was rocky, but it had improved when he'd started to travel extensively for work, being a top executive at Boeing. But her relationship with her daughter had started to deteriorate long before her marriage ran its course.

For years, Bree put up with a lot. What she was going to wear to school, the way her hair would be styled, the way that she was expected to speak and act. Her mother saw Bree as an extension of herself. That meant that she had to present as someone who Mrs. Zander would not be embarrassed to call her daughter. She would never curse, never yell, never even raise her voice.

She would always look proper and say appropriate things. Sometimes, Bree wondered if her mother had lived in an entirely different universe from everyone else. Her mother tracked her every move and had for years, forcing Bree to become rather ingenious in her lies and secrets.

She knew that her diary would be read, so she kept two. She knew that her phone would be checked, and so she saved up from her allowance and bought an old iPhone 5 that worked well enough that she could make videos and everything else that she wanted. When the screen broke, she fixed it herself. When the camera finally gave out, she got a kit online and replaced it herself.

Unbeknownst to Mrs. Zander, Bree lived a whole different life online than she did at home. She bought some clothes in a thrift store and kept them hidden in a special compartment at the bottom of her dresser. She often left the house in something that met her mother's approval, and then changed into clothes that reflected her true self when she went to the bookstore.

The library and the bookstore were the two places where Mrs. Zander seemed to relax around her daughter being out in public and not monitor her so much. The better that Bree was at faking certain things, like making dinner and being polite to guests at her parents dinner parties, the more freedom she got. But unlike other kids who sometimes might drink or do drugs, Bree just used this space to escape into her own reality. She performed being the lonely girl on TikTok, listening to Taylor Swift's folk album and moaning for a lost love, which she never had in real life. Even though Bree was sixteen, her mother still treated her like she was ten. She wouldn't let her get her driver's license. She checked up on every friend that she had. What Bree didn't know was that this came from a place of utter anxiety.

Her mother didn't know anything about raising teenage girls except from her own experience. She wanted to desperately protect her one child from being taken advantage of by a boyfriend, just like she had been when she was a kid. She blamed her parents for letting her go to the party where it happened. For some reason, Mrs. Zander never blamed the boy who had forced himself on her and wouldn't take no for an answer. Of course, she never shared this with her daughter. It would make her too vulnerable.

It was a Friday afternoon. The first of many, when the facade between the real Bree and her alternate reality as Danny Blue would start to fall apart. Her mother had caught her. Her mother had gotten to the bookstore early and saw her talking to one of the clerks, an older guy, nineteen at most, who was telling her all about his passion for Marcel Proust.

Danny had talked to him on a number of other occasions. She followed him on Instagram and TikTok and he followed her back. Never knowing her by any other name than Danny. When her mother saw Bree flirting through the window, she waited for her to come out and get into her SUV before locking the doors and telling her that she was not allowed to go anywhere again for the foreseeable future.

Before hearing that she was forbidden from going to Raven's Books for at least a month, Bree had been riding a high, the euphoria of flirting with a guy who likes you back. Her mother's ban was like a punch in the gut. She couldn't handle the prospect of not seeing him again. She felt sick to her stomach. She was about to throw up and she started to cry uncontrollably.

"I did nothing wrong," she repeated over and over. "We're just friends. We talk about books."

"No, I think you come here to do more than that."

Mrs. Zander thrust her finger in her daughter's face.

"And I don't want that. He's older than you. He's going to take advantage."

"No, he won't!" Bree yelled, raising her voice enough to strain her vocal cords.

Her mother's eyes got big. This was the first time that her daughter had ever raised her voice to her. She hadn't even thought that it was possible.

"Fine. Is it okay if I go out with someone my own age then?"

"So, you don't really care about this guy? Do you?" her mom snapped. "You just want a guy; any guy will do?"

"What are you trying to say?" Bree yelled. "That's you, twisting my words around. Everyone at school is dating and hanging out. I don't know what your problem is."

"My problem is that men can't be trusted, especially the guys that go to your school."

"Then why am I there? You're the one who chose it. You're the one who is paying all this money to send me there." Bree was angry.

Then she regretted immediately bringing up her school because, in reality, she liked it a lot. She liked her teachers. She liked her small classes, and her mother was all wrong about the boys that went there. The public school kids were way worse.

The fight continued about the guy who worked at the bookstore and about everything else. By the time that Bree was back in her room, she knew that something was going to change. That something *needed* to change.

She had made some plans. She had put some money away, but nothing major. She wondered if she had enough. When she counted it up, it was barely $400 and she knew she needed more.

Would her mother cut back her allowance just like she did the last time they had an argument? This wasn't the first fight, but it was the biggest. There had been other rumblings. It was only to be expected. When you clamp someone down so hard and you put them in a little cage and watch their every move, eventually they are going to start throwing themselves against the bars.

Mrs. Zander did not know this, though. She never cared about reading any of the books that her mother-in-law got her about raising teenagers and kids before that. After all, her mother-in-law had raised the man she was married to and he was no prize. Besides, Mrs. Zander thought that those books did not hold any special knowledge. She believed that she, as a mother, knew best.

When her father came home, Bree cried and yelled for him and told him everything that had happened. But like always, he deferred to her mother. He said that he wasn't there enough to watch her and that her mother was doing her best. He always sided with her mother, and Bree hated him for it.

He didn't know about the stalking that she had endured and didn't seem interested in getting involved. When she did bring it up to him, he just looked at her. She told him about her mother reading her diaries, stalking her online, and everything else but her father refused to believe her. But she kept pressing, trying to make him understand. She didn't have any other choice.

"Look, whatever your mother is doing she's doing it for your own good. If she's reading your diary, she's just trying to keep you safe. I would do the same thing," he said.

But that was a lie. Her father couldn't care less.

"What she should be doing is keeping tabs on you," Bree finally snapped, and her father's eyes got wide and big.

His daughter had never spoken to him like this, and for a second he felt a pang of fear.

"What are you talking about?" He lowered his voice, knowing exactly what she was referencing.

"You know what. Other women. I used to think there was just one girl but there are more, aren't there? Where do you meet them all or are they all escorts?"

He raised his hand and slapped her across the mouth. Unlike her mother, he had never hit her before, but he had seen it done plenty of times.

Bree yelped in pain and grabbed onto her face as her father turned around and stormed off. When her mom came into her room an hour later to comfort her, Bree took the food and told her to get out. For some reason, Mrs. Zander listened.

Things had gone too far, and no one knew how to step back off the cliff. With her face still throbbing and her body full of humiliation and sadness, Bree packed a small bag with only her thrift store clothes, a few other belongings, and an old tent that her mom had gotten her for a second grade Girl Scout trip that she had volunteered for as well.

The door to her room was naturally locked so she didn't bother trying it. Instead, she cracked her window open and waited to hear if anyone was awakened by the little beep. Then she took off the screen and climbed out.

9

Bree

When she jumped out of her window, her heart was beating a thousand times a minute. Her room was on the second story, but there was a section of roof over the porch. She climbed down using the branches of the tree that she had swung from on a tire swing as a kid. This was one of the few indulgences her father had allowed despite her mother's protests. She was too worried about her skinning a knee or smashing her face or even spraining an ankle. That would have made her ineligible to participate in various pageants and dance competitions.

Flashes of those past events came to her unbidden. The stress and anxiety, her mother's disappointment, all rushed in and formed a knot in her stomach. Bree pushed those thoughts out of her mind and focused on the present.

She ran hard and fast down the street of her bedroom community where people often walked their dogs late at night after their long commutes home from their jobs at Microsoft and Boeing. There were two gates securing access to the community about two miles apart, each with a pedestrian door that you could exit through. Thankfully, no cameras were set up to monitor who was coming in or out.

Every car had to come in with a transponder or call the house to someone inside the community to open it. As a result, it never occurred to anyone at the HOA to set up cameras to watch the gate because no one ever really walked in or out of it. Outside of the community was a busy road, people driving sixty, seventy miles an hour and no shops or stores within miles. But Bree, who wasn't allowed to drive, knew one thing. She knew the bus schedule, and she had taken it on a few occasions just to learn how to do it. She'd never planned on running away.

But she's glad that she had tried it out and that this wouldn't be her first time on public transport. The bus stop was a quarter mile down the four-lane road that was filled with speeding cars around the morning and afternoon commutes, but was almost abandoned this late in the evening.

The bus would come even at night. She had checked the schedule on her secret phone so that her steps could not be tracked by her parents. She knew that the bus wasn't coming for forty-five minutes so she took her time walking.

Occasionally a few headlights came from behind her, the light wrapping around her like a wave, throwing a sharp shadow in front of her. She decided not to worry about whether it was her parents who were coming but instead deal with that issue if it were to arise. Besides, she wouldn't be able to tell what car it was in the pitch blackness anyway. There were big shrubs all along the road leading to the other communities and she made the decision to go and jump in there in case it was her parents who were trying to pull her over.

Sitting at the bus stop, she huddled into the corner and listened to music on her phone. The bus came as expected and she was the only one to get on. She paid in cash and took it to the end of the line, another nearby suburb where she waited again and switched to the one that was heading down to Olympia but got off in Tacoma. She hadn't made any real plan. She considered riding the buses the whole night, waiting it out, but then looked up places to go for teenage runaways and saw a bunch of shelters listed in Seattle all the way down to Portland.

That's what she was now, she realized, a runaway. She wasn't sure how she felt about that.

Partly scared of course. She made a few videos and posted them on TikTok.

In the videos, she tried to express how she felt with music and images, and this version of herself, Danny Blue, that her parents would never see. She didn't post for others. She posted purely for herself but the few times that she got some comments back, she suddenly felt like there was a real connection made with people who understood.

She had decided against going to Seattle because she figured that her money wouldn't last as long there. There were already a lot of home-less youths there and she was worried about getting mugged. She was a sheltered rich kid after all, and up until this point, the most transgressive thing that she'd done was talk to a guy who worked in a bookstore. Where would her life lead now? She wondered and worried, but she couldn't wait to find out.

She rode two more buses. Once she got to Tacoma, she found a route for a bus that made a loop and rode it until the morning commute started. People had funneled on and she knew that this way, she would stand out less. What she really needed was a job before she started to look too much like the streets. She had seen the kids and the adults wandering around like *The Walking Dead,* dirty, disheveled, carrying large sacks full of the few possessions that they owned. This would probably happen to her.

A lot of the water in the parks had been turned off so that it wouldn't attract the undesirable element to bathe in the restrooms, and it would be only a day or two before her hair would get oily and gross, and she would look like someone who no one would want to hire. Her phone was running low on its charge. She had a backup battery, but she decided to head to a Barnes & Noble, recharge, grab something to drink, and have the protein bars that she had stashed in her room.

Ideally, this whole plan would be executed under much better circumstances, but beggars couldn't be choosers. She'd never ordered cold brew coffee before, but for some reason, it sounded good. She wasn't really a fan of coffee in general, but she also needed the caffeine after spending all night on various buses. She asked if she could return it if she didn't like it, and the Starbucks employee gave her a resounding yes.

"Yes, you can try whatever you want, and if you don't like it, we'll be happy to give you something else," she said with a smile.

A job here would be a dream and maybe she was old enough to work, but it would require her to give her social security number and some sort of ID, and would therefore be traceable. She didn't have her social security card with her, but she knew the number by heart. When her parents started to look for her, would they be able to check whether her social security number was getting pinged anywhere as an employee? She wasn't sure, but she knew that she had a good chance of getting a judge to grant her emancipation as a child if she had a job and looked like someone who was a respectable member of society.

Thanks to her mother, Bree didn't have many friends, sleepovers and lots of parties were forbidden. But that also meant that she didn't now turn to any of them to give her shelter. That would make her way too easy to find.

Would it even occur to them that she would try to find a job? Bree wasn't sure, but she knew one thing: Google was her friend and she would learn as much as she could on how to live on her own in the next few hours that she had in this warm, cozy place surrounded by books.

10

Bree

Bree couldn't find any conclusive information about whether someone could track her social security number without access to law enforcement databases, but she knew that she needed a place to sleep. First, she needed a job to make sure that she could afford it. She'd be comfortable spending $100 on a hotel room if she knew that she wouldn't have to move out completely penniless in less than a few more days. Barnes and Noble didn't have any openings, but the friendly clerk out front asked her if she knew about the new place that had just opened around the corner, a couple of blocks away.

"It's an indie bookstore and they sell a mixture of new and used books. I know they had a help wanted sign out in the window for quite some time. You may want to check out that place." Bree smiled.

She followed the clerk's directions and headed straight there. It was mid-morning and the place was deserted except for a woman in her fifties who gave her a big smile as soon as she entered.

"Welcome to the Book Nook."

"Let me know if I can help you find anything specific or just enjoy browsing."

"Thanks," Bree said, and suddenly felt very shy about coming right up to her and asking for a job. Instead, she browsed a little bit, looking through her usual favorites, young adult romance, young adult fantasy romance, and the like. This place had a coffee shop in the back which she saw when she was walking by the nonfiction section. The pastries looked to die for and said that they were from a local bakery.

Finally, summoning enough courage, she decided to head back to the front.

"Hi, excuse me. Are you the owner?"

"Yes, I am. We just opened. I'm so excited to have you here."

"Congratulations." Bree smiled. "I was just wondering if you were possibly looking for any help. I love books. I read a lot of them. I just moved to this area, so I need a part-time job."

The woman extended her hand and introduced herself as Frances Meeks. "My husband

and I started this place because, well, it's always been a dream of ours to open a cafe bookstore. He loves coffee and we both love books. We finally got the money together and decided to just jump into it."

Bree wasn't sure what to say, but she smiled, nodded, and told her good luck.

"Tell me about you, what's your name?"

Her heart skipped a beat. She wasn't sure what to say. What would be appropriate? Should she lie? Then if she had to submit her social security card, Mrs. Meeks would for sure find out the truth.

"I'm Danny," Bree said, extending her hand. "Danny Lofton. I just moved here with my parents, so I don't know the area very well."

"What grade are you in?"

"Tenth."

"New school?"

"Yes, we weren't living that far, up in Redmond, but something to do with my dad's job, we had to come here."

"Oh, no, I totally understand that. I moved around a lot as a kid."

Bree and Frances chatted a little bit and Bree could tell immediately that Frances was her kind of woman. She was easygoing, unassuming, unpretentious. The books that were stocked were both literary and popular, traditionally published and independent. She liked the inclusivity of the place.

"So to be honest with you," Frances said after she'd treated Bree to two cups of iced tea and a bagel with cream cheese, "we weren't thinking of hiring anyone for a while. I mean, it's a small place. We thought we'd save the money on staff, but I like you."

"If you need any help with developing your social media pages or your TikTok to bring in new readers, I can help with that," Bree said excitedly. "I know the kind of stuff that people post on Book Tok. The kinds of things that are expected, you know?"

"Yes. That's good to hear. Well, I have to discuss this with my husband, but would twenty hours a week work for you? I know you'll be going to school, so the hours would be in the afternoons and weekends."

"That's perfect!" Bree smiled widely. She felt like she was beaming like things make sense now that hadn't earlier.

"Now, would you mind if I paid you cash for a little while before I have all the payroll and everything set up? I don't know. We never ran a business like this before, you know, with employees, so I don't know the details of all of that."

"Of course. You should take your time. It's

really no big deal. I like cash," Bree said, trying to be a little bit sarcastic.

A wave of relief washed over Frances' face.

While whatever business that allowed her to buy this place was probably successful enough, she did seem to have a little bit of a fish out of water element to her. It must have been pretty pronounced, Bree decided, if she, a sixteen-year-old, noticed.

Walking out of the bookstore, well-fed and hydrated, carrying the new Sarah Maas release which she didn't even have to pay for, Bree was on top of the world. In less than twenty-four hours, she had a job, and at thirteen dollars an hour cash, twenty hours a week. She had enough to actually go about finding some accommodations.

It didn't have to be fancy. It didn't have to be a hotel. Anything weekly or monthly would work. She just knew that it would all work out from now on.

Chapter 11

Luke drove after Trincia following close behind. Wherever he's headed, he's in a major hurry. The excitement of the chase gets to me, and I start imagining all the possible scenarios.

What if right now he's headed to some house in a suburban neighborhood where he's keeping someone hostage? What if the bodies are there? No, I realize that that can't be the truth. If these four bodies are connected to him, they were all found in heavily wooded areas, killed in different ways.

Does it mean that he doesn't keep the people in a secluded place first? Of course not. But that's probably not where we would find anyone unless they were alive. My imagination is running wild and that's the reader and the writer in me, rather than the detective. Anything is possible in a novel as long as the story is set up a particular way. The twists and the inevitabilities can all be explained.

But in this situation, it's different. David Trincia's not a character in a story. He may be rushing off to an appointment with a doctor. He may be late for a meeting with a client. There could be any number of reasons for him to rush away from his office, and here we are, three fools who are hanging onto his every move.

"Where is he going?" I keep asking out loud as he drives off the freeway and heads toward a national park. He stops short of the boundary. Instead, he takes one of the unpaved roads that leads deep into the forest. The car that was in front of him disappears further down the road.

Luke turns to me and asks, "Should we follow him?"

"It would be impossible to hide there," Donald says, pointing to the unpaved trail masquerading as the road. "If he sees us, the jig is up."

"He doesn't know who we are," I point out. "He's never seen you, right?"

"No. I used different cars the few times I followed him."

"There must be other people who live down this way."

"There are, but at least this car will be identified."

"Why don't you just follow him a little bit," I

say, "to see where he goes? We don't have to pull over, and if we feel like he might see us, we'll just turn away."

I hide my hair under a baseball hat and sunglasses despite the fact that I haven't seen the sun in days.

Donald tugs on the hood of my sweater and says, "Pull this up instead. It's hard to tell even your sex if you're wearing a hoodie and your hair is out of the way. The sunglasses are going to draw attention."

Luke follows far enough behind to avoid suspicion. David's car is driving through the mud out in the far distance. My only concern at this point, as my heart starts to speed up, is whether he's the only one who has property here, the only cabin, but this is a whole road and I'm hoping that's not the case. A few minutes later, I see houses show up, small wooden cabins with small lots and then, a little bit out in the distance, it's a clear lot for a mini mansion with tall, sky-high windows looking out into the forest and the meadow in front of it.

"Okay. We're not the only ones here." I let out a sigh of relief, and so does everyone else.

The silence is deafening.

Luke had turned off the music and all we hear is the squish of the mud and the crunch of rocks and dirt underneath the car's tires. Then out in the distance, there's a T in the road. I try to look on Google maps, but I'd lost reception a long time ago.

David's car disappears. He must have turned left or right, but which one?

"When we get to the T," Luke turns to me and asks, "which way?"

I peek out the window and out by a cabin far, far to the right, I feel like I see his silver BMW. All the other cars around here are a dark color, so his kind of stands out. Luke looks on his phone's GPS, which is still miraculously working, zooms in close, and we both see that the road ends at that cabin.

"If I drive further and we get closer, he'll see the license plate. Who knows where we can turn around?"

"What do we do? Just leave it like this?" I ask.

"He's there now, right? Let me drive a little bit closer but we're definitely switching cars. We all cover our faces just in case there are any cameras or anything set up."

I even pull down the visor on the front seat.

Luke drives up a little bit closer where we can get a clear shot of his car, the one we were following all along, parked in front of a small A-frame cabin surrounded by woods. The cabin isn't really a house. I doubt that it's more than one bedroom, maybe two if you count the loft up top. I've seen numerous places like this back in the mountains around Big Bear and had gotten used to gauging their size based on their outside dimensions.

"I've got to turn around here if we don't want him to see. He may have a telescope, who knows? We're just out in the clear."

"Yes."

"What about getting out?" I ask.

For a second, I refer to Donald. He's the one who's most experienced, and frankly most invested in this case.

"If we get out and walk around, we probably won't see anything," he says.

"What if he sees our car and then moves it anyway?" I ask.

"We don't have a warrant. We're not going to get one. Our best bet is just to turn around now, look like some people lost driving through the woods, and come back maybe when he's not here."

This sends a cold chill through my body. This whole time, I was waiting for evidence but what if he is keeping someone here? Hurting someone?

"You know that our best bet is to walk around that place," I say, "and if we hear any screams or anything else, we have exigent circumstances."

"You don't even have jurisdiction here," Luke says. "If you go in there, you could ruin the chain of evidence and the DA will have nothing to pin on him. He could skate on everything because you have no investigatory authority. Our best bet is to try to find something that will convince the local authorities to investigate, something that doesn't require us either tipping him off or creating a 'fruit of the poisonous tree' situation."

"No, we should—" I start to say.

"No, I'm going to turn around now. I'm going to wait out there, wait for him to pull out and leave."

"What if he kills someone now?" I ask.

"We can't sacrifice all of this on an if, we've already gone too far." Luke puts it in perspective.

I'm not really on the side of breaking in. In fact, if one of them were saying it, I'd probably be arguing the opposite. It's good to know that we all have one goal in mind. Besides, we have no proof that this place is anything but his second home, a place to get away where nothing bad happens.

Luke turns around and pulls away, turning left at the T and toward the end of the road.

I t would be an understatement to say that I was disappointed that we were leaving the cabin, but I knew there was no other way around it. If he had seen us, gotten suspicious, the whole thing would blow up in our faces. The element of surprise and the fact that David Trincia doesn't know that anyone's watching him is the one thing we have going for us because, frankly, there's nothing else.

Nevertheless, it's hard to describe the disappointment of being so close to finding out something and then not getting your way. If this were an official tail, and we had permission from local law enforcement, it would be different. Someone would sit here in another unmarked car, maybe position themself in a nearby cabin but none of that is authorized. As private investigators working for no pay, resources are slim. Yet my hopes remain high until I get a phone call. It's Captain Carville. It's unusual to get a call from him, so I show it to everyone while I answer.

"Just wanted to reach out to you and let you know that it looks like the wife is going to renege on the alibi."

"You mean Cora's ex-husband's new wife?" I ask.

"Yes. We're talking to her now. Nothing official yet, but she's pretty shook up over the affair. Don't know why, their relationship started as an affair. As the saying goes, if they'll do it with you, they'll do it to you, but I guess people have to learn their own lessons. I'll let you know what happens but if that alibi falls, he's our guy. You know that, right?"

"Yes, of course."

"Now, I'm not saying that you're totally off course here, but it should be a relief to you if the ex-husband did it. It's a simpler case to solve, it's obvious and it's not related to this supposed serial killer that you and I both know is highly unlikely."

"Of course. I really appreciate you reaching out. I know you didn't have to, so thank you."

He hangs up. I relay the news. The three of us aren't sure where to go from here.

"Him being connected to the Cora murder is a long shot," Luke says.

"I knew that all along," I say.

"I mean the ex-husband or the new boyfriend are the obvious choices. I thought that they had ruled them out, but things have changed."

"It could still be significant," Donald says.

I turned to face him.

"It could also be nothing. We could be grasping at straws, following some guy to his hunting cabin or whatever that is, wasting our time. I'm not mad at you, I'm just frustrated over the whole thing because the truth is that we don't have the resources here. All three of us could be watching him day and night taking shifts for weeks on end and get nothing. We have no idea how he operates. We just have a confession from a dubious source, a new friend of yours who may be just wanting to impress you."

"You can't believe that," Donald says. "I don't

know about Cora, but the other three are his. Victor didn't want to tell me any of that stuff and he did it in confidence. He was shook up over it, don't you see?"

I can't help but agree. When I talked to Victor, I didn't get a sense that he was lying at all.

"Let's just take a break," I say. "We're probably going to stay in the hotel down here if you want to take the car back up, and then come down tomorrow. But I need a little break."

"I don't want to make the drive back and then drive down again, so I'll stay here overnight. I have a few things with me."

I give him a nod. Something about Donald staying at our hotel makes me feel a little bit uncomfortable but there's no good alternative. I just want to get out of here, take a shower, and clear my head. Hopefully, the place has a gym. The rain had started up again and sitting here for so long has made my whole body stiff.

12

Frieda

She didn't know where to begin. She didn't know how it had gotten so bad, but it had. One moment, he was her boyfriend and then, after an hour-long discussion over coffee at a campus Starbucks, he wasn't. What had happened? How did the whole world shift underneath her feet so quickly without any warning? Is that possible?

Taylor Watkins was the popular guy on campus. A graduate student in biomedical engineering who ran cross country on the club team. He even had time to work in student government. He was exactly the kind of guy that she would've never dated in high school. But when he showed interest in her, she decided to say yes. Why not? She was old enough now, twenty-five, a graduate student herself in mathematics. Only she wasn't as bright now as she was in college and high school.

Everyone else seemed to get the material much faster, didn't seem to struggle so much with teaching classes.

Frieda and Taylor had dated for over a year and a half. The first couple of months, she couldn't believe that he was actually interested, but then she got used to it. They spent all their time together. She would visit him and hang out with his roommates, listen to banter about football and try to keep up. He would often stay over at her place because she lived alone in a studio.

The talk that he had with her at Starbucks had come out of the blue. Nothing seemed to be different since this weekend. They hung out, went to a party, made love afterward, everything was normal, or so she thought.

Was that just mercy sex? Frieda tried to remember if she had initiated it or him, but they'd both had a little bit too much to drink, fell into bed, and it just sort of happened. Had she been obtuse this whole time? Had she not noticed the signs of him pulling away?

He was studying a lot. One of the classes he was taking, biomedical fundamentals was kicking his butt. He was naturally smart, and things had always come easy for him, but this professor didn't find him as charming as perhaps others did. That was all it was, right? He was frustrated.

"Listen, I've been thinking about this for a while and I need some space," Taylor said.

"You mean you want to sleep over less?" she asked innocently, taking a sip of her latte.

"No, I think we should take a break."

"From what?"

"From us."

She understood the word break and she knew all its connotations, but it had never been applied to her. She had never had a long-term relationship like this. If he needed more time, they could see each other less, but what's the point of this?

"Why do you need a break?" she asked instead. "We can just see each other a little less. You can just study more. We don't have to meet up so much."

"Are you going to really force me to say this?" Taylor leaned over his coffee cup, whispering.

He had planned this, she realized at that moment. He knew that she had her class in an hour, and this conversation would be limited by that. He didn't do this in person at night when it could go on for hours. Instead, he wanted to meet in this public place. Everything about this was orchestrated.

"Look, I don't think I'm in the right head space to have a girlfriend. I love you, but I really need to focus on my classes, and I don't want the added pressure."

"What pressure?" she asked.

He seemed annoyed and huffed in response.

"I'm sorry about all the questions, but this is coming out of nowhere. Everything was fine, right?"

He shrugged.

"We argued a little, but I don't understand where this is coming from," she added.

She tried to ease her tone of voice. She didn't want to accuse him of anything. She was afraid he would start to pull away. What she didn't know was that he was already long gone. Taylor had checked out a month ago and had just postponed the inevitable because he didn't want to hurt her feelings.

"We haven't seen each other that much recently. Maybe we should work on this."

"No, I don't want to." Taylor shook his head, exasperated.

This was going worse than he had imagined. Part of the problem was that this was brand new information to Frieda, but it was something that he had thought about and mulled over for a while. He looked at the time, twenty minutes left. He'd give her that much, answer her questions, and then be on his way.

"Look, if I'm pressuring you to see me too much, we can do less. I just don't see why we have to break up. I think we have a really good thing here," Frieda said, trying to contain her composure, but her hands were beginning to tremble. "We were really good together, Taylor, you know that, right?"

"You're really going to make me say it. Really?"

"Say what?"

"I don't feel the same way anymore. I haven't felt the same way in months."

"But we just had sex."

"That's just sex." He shakes his head. "I love you as a friend, and what we had was special, but I just kept thinking, where is this going? Do I want to spend the rest of my life with you? I don't know. I don't think so. I don't think I'm ready for that."

"I'm not pressuring you about that at all," Frieda said. "Have I brought up getting married once or even moving in together?"

"No, you haven't, but relationships have to go somewhere. Otherwise, what's the point?"

"So, you're just breaking up with me because you're not ready to get married?"

"I'm not ready to be in a relationship. I want to date around. I want to meet new people. Everything in my life is serious enough."

Frieda's heart tightened. She knew that his parents were going through a bad divorce, and they were putting him in the middle of it. His father had found a new girlfriend. His mother had found out that his father had been cheating for years, and Taylor had been forced to become the mediator between the two.

No amount of money was enough for his mother, but now that the kids were grown up, she was looking at getting nothing because she had signed a prenuptial agreement when she was twenty-two. She probably wouldn't even get the house. That made his mom, who had devoted her whole life to her family and her children and had medical issues to boot, insanely frustrated and angry.

"Look, I know you're going through a lot with your parents and your degree, but you don't have to take it out on me. I could be a support system for you. I could be your rock. You can talk to me about everything."

"I don't want to talk to you about everything. You know what I want to do right now?"

"What?"

He motions to the slim blonde barista with tattoos up and down her arms and charcoal around her lower eyelids.

"I want to go over and talk to her. I want to get her number. I want to spend a night with her and never call her again and not cheat on you."

"You're a pig," Frieda said.

"No." Taylor frowned, getting frustrated. "I just don't want to be serious. That's what I'm trying to tell you as a friend. You did nothing wrong. I did nothing wrong. I don't want to get to the point like my father, where I cheat on you just to get away. I'm being honest about what I want, and I'm sorry that inconveniences you. I'm sorry for hurting your feelings, but I'm just not in a good head space for a relationship right now."

That was it. With that statement, he grabbed his backpack and phone and walked off. Frieda took the lid off her cup and stared into the bottom of her latte as if she were reading her fortune in tea leaves. Nothing came up. She didn't believe in that sort of thing anyway.

The tears didn't come until later, until she exited the coffee shop and the first drizzle hit her face. She let her tears flow and sobbed, wiping them only occasionally, knowing that in the rain, people couldn't really see that you're crying anyway. She pulled the hood over her head. Her waterproof jacket was keeping her dry inside, but her face was drenched and so were her hands, freezing in the cool air.

She didn't go to her teaching assistant job that afternoon. Whenever she wasn't available, she was supposed to call the office assistant of the mathematics department, Cheryl, who took care of all the professors and all the teaching assistants, organized the schedules, assigned substitutes, printed conference materials, and even mothered them through bad relationships, everything that was above and beyond the scope of her job description.

Everyone in the department saw Cheryl, a woman in her early sixties, as a motherly comforting type and the new batches of graduate students quickly learned to rely on her for whatever help they needed with any administrative tasks. But Frieda never felt comfortable. No matter how many times Cheryl had offered her help, she would politely decline, instead doing most of her preparations herself.

Despite this, Cheryl had never been alienated. She had worked in the math department for over thirty years and had met many aloof and closed-off personalities over that time; math people are not known to have the best communication skills. She knew that her job was just to be there and to offer help, and she would be taken up on that opportunity whenever it would be needed.

If Frieda had gone to the department to tell her that she couldn't teach that afternoon or even called her on the phone, Cheryl would have immediately known that something traumatic had happened and gone out of her way to find a substitute or, as a last resort, show up to the classroom herself and tell the students waiting that the session was going to be made up at a later time.

But Frieda couldn't bring herself to call. She

couldn't stop crying, and she was afraid that if she were to utter a word, she would break down completely.

Instead, she walked. She made loops around campus. When the rain got worse, she went inside the bookstore and wandered around there looking mindlessly at fantasy romance books which she used to devour as a teenager.

13

Frieda

Frieda desperately wanted to be somewhere else, to be someone else, to numb all the pain, but she couldn't. Instead, she cowered in the comic book section and cried softly until a couple of thirteen-year-olds came around and gave her weird looks. Finally, she decided to head home. She usually took the bus, but she walked past the stop and decided to go on foot. It was about a thirty-minute walk, but it took her forty-five because she walked so slowly, distracted, waiting too long at crosswalks, letting the lights turn a few times before going, and feeling sorry for herself.

When she climbed the steps to her second-floor apartment, a small studio sparsely decorated, she peeled off her wet coat, hung it up near the door letting the mat underneath soak up the water. She put her boots to the side and peeled off

122

all of her clothing, throwing it into the garbage rather than the hamper, knowing that the outfit had been damned somehow. The jeans and the red blouse, her favorite unfortunately, were now forever linked to the breakup, and they were like the black suit that you wear to a funeral once that you can never muster the desire to wear again.

She put on her favorite pair of cotton, over-sized pajama bottoms, and a t-shirt. She opened one of the cabinets that was serving as a pantry and grabbed a Kraft macaroni and cheese, popping it into the microwave. This has been her comfort food for two weeks now and she needed it more than ever. When it came to nutrition, she wasn't the best. She would eat the same thing over and over again until she got sick of it, even if it took months.

The types of foods she ate were very limited, primarily carbs and cheese. Her favorites were frozen concoctions from Trader Joe's, the one store that she could afford to shop in and feel as though her refrigerator was full. Her childish palate had annoyed Taylor, who grew up eating foie gras and knew that white wine was paired with fish at fourteen. He enjoyed going to fancy restaurants and popups and trying food combinations that didn't make any sense to Frieda like fig and bacon. The idea of it made her stomach turn.

Frieda Wolfe was just a girl from a small town

known for sweet onions. She had lived in Walla Walla, Washington, her whole life, born and raised on a hobby farm. Her parents loved animals, had them for no other reason than to enjoy them. She grew up riding her horse, playing with chickens, and eating macaroni and cheese and pancakes on Sundays. Her parents, who both only had a high school education, were kind, church-going people, who didn't judge and didn't like to be judged.

They took in an exchange student from Nigeria her junior year. Frieda still missed her and kept in touch with her even after she'd gone to Oxford for her university studies. In fact, it was this Nigerian exchange student who had inspired her to go to college and graduate school. She was the only one Frieda knew who had big dreams and aspirations, and just knowing that she existed made Frieda believe that she could have them, too.

Her parents were, of course, supportive but cautious; not knowing that there was anything a person could do with a math degree besides become a math teacher or an engineer. After she got her bachelor's degree from Whitman College while living at home, Frieda decided to apply to University of Washington in Seattle for her graduate studies, as well as Berkeley, a couple of other University of California schools, and Portland

State. The University of Washington gave her the best tuition care package. Plus, she had only been to Seattle once before on a weekend trip and had been dreaming of living in the big city ever since.

She had been there almost two years and she had been struggling for as long. The other graduate students had come from other places, many had gone to international boarding schools, all had lived on campus in college, and had been on their own for what seemed like years at that point. It was easy for them to make friends, to meet up, to connect with others in the department, but it wasn't easy for Frieda. Even the ones with limited social skills somehow flourished because they could play League of Legends together and classics like GoldenEye for fun.

Frieda wasn't into video games and she felt like she had little in common with anyone, mostly because she didn't bother getting to know anyone. For some people, just being part of the same department would be enough, but at this point in her life, she thought that she actually had to have something in common with people to make a connection.

Frieda put on the TV and watched reruns of *Keeping up with the Kardashians*. She never told anyone in her life that she watched this show because it was not something that someone of her intellect and academic accomplishment was supposed to enjoy, but there was something easy-going, appealing, and nostalgic about it. Having been on for years, they were old, somewhat annoying characters that you vaguely knew of.

She wasn't a diehard fan who never missed an episode, she was someone who would put it on in the background and tried to do her combinatorics homework. On this particular night, she just watched the show and nothing else, letting it wash over her as she filled her belly with textured powdered cheese. The previously powdered cheese that had been melted over the macaroni that tasted exactly the same way it did when she was six years old.

When her mom called at seven that night, as she usually did every evening, she answered in her cheery friendly voice, revealing nothing of the breakup. She asked about the animals and how Chrissy, her old horse, was doing. Her arthritis was getting bad, but she was getting physical therapy from a new yoga teacher in town, a transplant from Seattle, who had moved to escape high rent and buy her own little plot of paradise here in Walla Walla. Frieda's mom had taken her under her wing. In return, her new friend had taught her how to do equine physical therapy. Her mom was worried about her daughter being so far away and she often brought up and made plans for the next time she would be home.

"I might come home earlier. I'm feeling a little bit tired of all the classes and everything and was thinking of maybe taking next week off."

"Oh, that would be wonderful, honey," her mom said, beaming on the other end. "I can make your favorite mile-high apple pie."

"That would be amazing." Frieda's mouth salivated.

"How's everything with school?"

"Good, hard." With this part of her life, Frieda was honest. Her mom knew that graduate school was not what she'd expected, but she wasn't sure if her daughter was suffering from imposter syndrome or whether she was actually inadequately prepared to be there.

"I just feel like everyone knows a lot more. Everything's easier for them."

"Have you been doing anything fun? Any nights out with friends?"

"No, not really."

For the longest time, she thought that she had enough friends. She had Taylor and he knew everybody and so there were parties to go to and people to talk to and then there was him to spend time with. But now it seemed like everything was different. Now, she realized that they were all his friends. She never really met up with anyone by herself. Now that she and Taylor were broken up, she had no one.

"How's Taylor? Still having trouble in that class?"

"Yes, he is but he's going to get through it. You know him."

"Of course."

Taylor had FaceTimed her parents numerous times and even came out for Christmas last year, the whole two weeks. They were fast friends because the Wolfes would have been happy with whomever their daughter would've brought home as long as he was loving toward her. Frieda couldn't bring herself to tell her mother about the breakup.

Her mother wouldn't judge. Her mother would understand. She wouldn't even call him names. She would be there for her in the way that anyone would want their mother to be there for them and yet Frieda was humiliated and sad, and that closed her off. She just couldn't bring herself to say anything. After talking about the new batch of chickens that were just born, Frieda hung up the phone, lay down on the couch, and let the blue glow of the television wash over her as she tried to fall asleep. Little did she know that this would be the last night that she would spend in her apartment and in less than twenty-four hours, she would never take another breath again.

Chapter 14

The motel room smelled like grits. I had been to the South once, and only just technically. I flew through the Atlanta airport on the way to Miami, which, even though it is geographically further south, is not capital 'S' Southern. It was lunchtime, I was hungry, so I decided to try the classic Southern breakfast: hushpuppies, fried green tomatoes, and grits, all the classics that I've read about in books and seen in movies, but never tasted myself.

The sweet tea was so sweet it almost made me gag. Fried green tomatoes were my favorites, with the hushpuppies a close second. You can't really go wrong with fried tomatoes and potatoes. The grits were odd in texture, smell, and composition, just little white dots, not pasta, not grain, salty and sweet at the same time. Perhaps I haven't tried the best kind. This wasn't a fancy Southern restaurant or anything like that, but it put me off the entire food group.

That was the first and only time I had encountered that smell, not a lot of grits on the West coast, until I walked into this sixty-dollar hotel room by the side of the highway with a Denny's attached on the end. After last night's accommodations, everything about this place was gross. It wasn't until we'd checked in and opened our suitcases and unpacked a little bit that I saw the hairs in the bathtub drain.

The water didn't go down at all and just pooled around your ankles when you showered. The glasses on the sink were splattered with someone else's water. The scent of the grits was distinct, and it permeated the room.

"Where is it coming from?" I ask Luke. "This is so bizarre."

"Maybe Denny's?"

"No, they don't serve anything like that. This isn't Waffle House."

"Does Waffle House serve grits?" he asks.

I shrug.

"How do you know that it's grits?"

"Because I remember the smell and I've never smelled anything else like it."

He shrugs. "I don't mind it," and lies down on the stained comforter trying to make himself

Girl Hunted

comfortable on the uneven mattress that sinks slightly in the middle.

"Why are we here?" I ask. "Donald wanted to stay here, but there must be a nicer place."

"I just thought it'd be weird for three of us traveling together to stay in different hotels."

"This is the outskirts of Portland, there are no five-star hotels here," I say, feeling irritated from the burden of the day. "But at least a Super 8 or some chain where there's some standard of cleanliness, not this place. This place is just called The Motel, they didn't even bother giving it a name."

"Look, it was here. I figured we can order some food from the Denny's next door."

I shake my head annoyed and frustrated, mostly with myself if I were being honest. I should have insisted, I should have told him that I can't get good sleep without having a good bed, which is partly true, but it's not just the hotel that I'm angry at. The whole day has left me unnerved.

I'm still in a threadbare towel standing on the carpet and wondering whether I should have brought flip-flops like I used to when I was in college to avoid getting meningitis. Then I see that there's water flooding from underneath the bathtub.

"This whole floor is wet," I say to Luke. "The tub is like leaking or something."

Now I'm standing in the filthy soapy water. It's

131

not so much where it's a torrent, but just a thin layer of liquid to make it feel extra gross, and then out of the corner of my eye, I see a cockroach sitting proudly underneath the sink. I yell for Luke and run into the room.

Luke grabs his shoe and does the boyfriend's duty of exterminating the bug.

"We have to switch rooms," I say. "This place is awful."

"No, I'm too tired. I don't want to pack up. I just want to get some food and go to bed."

"This place has cockroaches. The tub is over-flowing and it probably has bed bugs."

"Nope, I checked for those," Luke says, raising his finger. "I always do. I had a really bad infestation in college."

"But aren't cockroaches enough?"

"Come on, they're not going to bother you. Do you know that they're actually really clean as far as bugs go?"

I stare at him in disbelief.

"I don't even know what that means," I say. "Has there been some measurement of the cleanliness of various insects?"

"Actually, yes. Even though we're all very afraid of cockroaches, they're pretty harmless and they don't spread diseases."

"Ugh. I don't care about that." I roll my eyes

and refuse to sit on top of the comforter, which I doubt has been washed once in the last month.

The sheets are clean enough and actually crisp to the touch, so I put on my pajamas and slide in, hoping that I have enough protection on me and my clothes from this room to make it through the night. I plug in my phone and begin to check social media mindlessly as both of us talk about what we should order from Denny's, but neither of us makes a move. They don't deliver. If we make an order, we'd have to go over there and pick it up.

Luke offers to do it, but I can tell that he's super tired. I can barely move. As frustrated as I am by this room and by the whole day in general, I end up falling asleep. The few times I wake up, my stomach is growling. I drink a couple of glasses of sink water and then force myself to go back to sleep.

In the morning, Luke and I both wake up early, it's barely five but we head straight to Denny's. Sipping a mug of thin, flavorless coffee, I collect my thoughts about our whole excursion up here.

"When I got the extension from my real job, I thought that ten days would be enough. At this point, I'm not sure it can be accomplished in months. And, you're not even supposed to be here much longer either," I say, looking over the giant menu and deciding on a loaded veggie omelet with a short stack of buttermilk pancakes.

"I got this text last night from Captain Carville." I hand Luke my phone. "It's a confirmation that the ex-wife, Melinda Rydell, says that Steven was not with her that night and he was out with his girlfriend after all."

"So, ex-husband is in play now?" Luke asks. I nod.

"He seems to be a much better suspect than before. I mean, they haven't been married for years, but I guess he's just that kind of a possessive asshole. He wanted to control her every move. I guess when she dated the other people, he didn't think it was serious but with Steven, maybe it was."

"You changed your mind just like that?" Luke asks.

His nine grain pancakes arrive first, and he digs in, motioning for me to grab my fork and take a bite, too. He puts a generous amount of syrup on top as well as some whipped cream and I take a big bite with great appreciation.

"I guess Melinda was going to give him an alibi as long as she didn't know that he was cheating on her. Now things are up in the air."

"So, you think the department has it handled?"

"I mean, better than we do. They are in a

position to get answers from him. You know what? I hope it is the ex-husband. It makes the most sense. It's the easiest case to make and as long as it's true. That's what her son thinks as well, right?"

"What about the red purse?" Luke asks.

I shrug.

"They made more than one. That's enough doubt right there. You don't seem like you agree."

"No, actually, I do." He chews with his mouth closed and washes it down with some coffee.

"I'm not sure the Cora case is connected to the other ones. We have nothing besides the purse anyway. We have no idea if that locket that she supposedly kept in it is there."

"We can't just leave Donald hanging, especially since he knows that we took the extra days off," Luke says.

"But things have changed. This case that I was a part of is no longer connected to the others, which themselves may or may not be connected to each other. I don't know if I want to waste what precious little time off I have to just sit in a car. It's something that he can do by himself. You know that I'm going to have to put in hours and hours of overtime to make up for all of this. And if it's a serial killer case, it's going to take years of actual police work to collect evidence. I'm not sure that Donald is in a position to do that anyway. Maybe we can investigate it later when I retire."

Luke nods. He doesn't say much, and I keep talking, covering the same thing over and over again, trying to convince myself, and him, that this is the right thing to do. For a bit there, as I eat the onions and slurp up the cheese from my omelet, I think that he disagrees, that he's going to make a valiant effort to convince me to stay, but he doesn't. There's a resignation there.

The text from Carville has changed a lot. He and I both know that.

With our bellies stuffed, we return to our room, hang out for a few hours, and then around nine, call Donald, but he doesn't answer.

I go to knock on his door. Again, no response.

He gave me one of his room keys, but when I let myself in, I see that he has checked out.

Chapter 15

"Donald is not here." I return to our room perplexed, not quite believing what I had just said myself. Luke tilts his head.

"What are you talking about?"

I shrug my shoulders uncertain as to how to make it any clearer.

"I let myself in and he's not there."

I pick up my phone and call his number. No one answers.

"He's just gone. No suitcase, nothing, just cleared out."

"He wouldn't do that," Luke says. "He's probably going to get back to us soon."

Uncertain as to what to do, I go out to the parking lot but the sounds of the highway and the stream of commuting cars annoys me, so I go back inside. It's overcast again and there's only a small window out front and the fluorescent lights inside make me want to crawl out of my skin. When Luke goes to brush his teeth and flips on the overhead above the sink, I avert my eyes.

I scroll through some social media as I let my mind wander. Where did he go and with what car? The rental is still parked out front. Suddenly my phone rings, his name pops on the screen.

"Hey, where are you?" I ask.

"I couldn't wait. I had to see what was here," Donald says. "I'm at the cabin, you have to come."

"What are you talking about? Weren't you in the room last night?"

"I left soon after, rented a car, came here, and staked out this place the whole night."

"And?" I ask.

"Trincia finally left at five AM. Hasn't been back so I've been walking around, and I found something. At least I think so. Come back. Park as far away as you can just because your car's been here already. I'll be waiting."

The cryptic message leaves me hanging.

I repeat it to Luke who just shrugs and says, "I guess we're going to the cabin again."

In the drive over, my stomach is in knots. It could be the big breakfast or maybe it's the anticipation of what it is exactly that Donald found.

The second time around, the road seems longer, more isolated but we know where we're going. The little bit of drizzle has cleared out and now it's just like parchment paper hanging over the pines. The white light makes it neither morning or evening, day or night.

We park by the side of the road in a dead-end, unpaved little trail with a 'No Trespassing' sign up front. Luke pulls the car over as much as he can, hopefully leaving enough room for someone else to drive through if need be. The last thing I want is to be this exposed, but it's still going to be quite a slog to get to the cabin even from out here.

"Should we hide the car more?" I ask.

He shrugs. "I wonder if that's just going to draw more attention to it."

He's right. This way, it looks like maybe we ran out of gas. This is a plausible explanation.

What happens if you come upon a car covered in leaves and tree branches that has been purposely placed there?

I'm thankful for my waterproof boots because the ground is soggy, water-logged. I tuck my jeans into the tops to make sure that the mosquitoes and the bugs don't fly up and bite me.

We walk for a while down a relatively empty road but luckily no cars pass. There are a few houses here, but they're set far away from the road and I have no way of knowing if anyone is inside watching.

I have a story set up though; we ran out of

gas, new people in town, just visiting and passing through thinking that this way would be the best way to get to the nearest gas station.

Finally, out on the horizon, I see the outline of the cabin. There's no car up front and I wonder where Donald has put it. Luke and I don't say much. Even though my night sleep wasn't very restful, the big breakfast in my stomach has improved my mood considerably as well as my outlook on the possibilities of this case.

My phone has no reception now. I keep forgetting because I play with it and keep it on for entertainment value. In times like this when I'm tense and anxious, I like to tune the world out, pop in my AirPods, put on an audiobook, and let someone else's story and someone else's thoughts drown out my own.

"I can't believe you're just going to check out. Aren't you nervous? What do you think he's found?" Luke asks, watching me.

"I have no idea what he found but we're not talking so I figured I'd just listen to something."

He shakes his head.

"Hey, listen, I do the same thing at the dentist. I don't like the sound of the drill on my teeth, shaking my whole head so I have something and let my thoughts go elsewhere."

"Wow, I didn't know this about you." I shrug.

"There are actually a lot of things you don't know."

He smiles.

"Let me try it." He reaches into his pocket and pops in one of his Google Pixel Buds. A few seconds later I see him bopping his head, rocking out to something he saved on his Spotify playlist.

"You know, this *is* better. It cuts you off from thinking so much," he says a little bit louder.

I smile and give him a wink. This is how we walk the rest of the way.

Finally, the cabin comes into view. Thick brown-orange pieces of lumber are carefully stacked with a lot of love and care to form this A-frame house. It's not spacious or ostentatious but it's beautiful. Nothing cheap or crappy about it.

Cabins like this don't come with garages and many people either forget to build one or don't have the finances to invest in one, leaving all of their tools, supplies in various sheds or all around the property. This one has neither the garage nor the clutter. At least not one visible from the road.

I have no way to confirm whether Donald is here because I have no reception. Luke still does and I think Donald might since he called me from here. Instead of heading straight up the makeshift driveway, I go around the circle. We make a big loop like we're just heading into the woods for a stroll. Out back, I spot a small shed and Donald standing on a rock trying to make his phone work.

"Hey!" Luke yells in a whisper, nearly as loud as if he had simply spoken.

Donald sees us and waves us over. There's a big smile on his face.

"How long have you been here?" I ask.

"Since last night. I didn't want to put you out. I knew you needed some rest, but I just couldn't let it go. I wanted to take a look around the cabin."

"Where's the car?" Luke asks.

"I parked it far back near the road. It's just one way in and one way out. Hiked in through the forest. Got lost for a bit, but then found my way. Waited out there in the woods," he points to kind of the direction from which we came, "until he left around five AM."

"What if he hadn't left?"

"I'd still be there." He shrugs. "You're right. I should have done all this myself earlier and not relied on you two." We look around. Nothing seems out of the ordinary.

"Have you been inside?" I whisper. He shakes his head no.

"But I looked in all the windows. Lights are off, pretty clean, put away. Looks like he left for a while or maybe he's just a neat freak. Who knows?"

I try to recollect the image of his main house. It was pretty clean. Everything put away just so.

"What is it that you wanted to show us?" I ask.

"I was walking around the property, really looking at the ground," he says. "Follow me."

We take about twenty steps in a northeast direction away from the shed. Right there just behind the pine trees, there's a grove, and a little disturbance in the ground. It's no bigger than three or four feet.

Donald points to it.

"What does this look like?" he asks.

The only thing that comes to mind is a grave. But it's not big enough for an adult.

Chapter 16

The terrain is notably irregular and markedly fresher than the surrounding grove, with no resemblance to the delicate greenery, moss, and thin grass that adorn the rest of the area. Though the soil has been carefully leveled, it is not entirely flawless. A slight bump in the earth implies that the ground was initially tough and rocky to excavate. While there are no visible markings, a discernible imprint or partial footprint to the side suggests that it has been disturbed before.

"You really think this is a grave?" Luke asks. I'm glad that he's taking the position of the skeptical one.

"Doesn't it look like it?" Donald asks.

"Even if it is, it's about three and a half feet, small. It could be a dog," Luke offers.

"I think the question is not so much what is in

there, but what do we do with it?" I say. "There's no way for us to know for sure until we dig it up, disturb it in any way, and then if we do find a child and we don't have a warrant, what happens?"

"We're not the police," Donald says. "We could just have found it."

"How? How could we have just found it? We were walking by?" I kicked it, saw something.

"We can come up with something," Donald says.

"But everyone knows that you've been trailing this guy everywhere, and then you happen to be the one that just happens to kick something up and find a grave? That's never going to stand up in court. He's going to hire a lawyer and get it all thrown out."

"Why are you thinking about court?" Donald snaps.

"Because that's all that matters. It's not about what we know. It's about what we can prove. We know lots of things. I could have just broken into his room, taken pictures, really searched it, and then what? What's the point of knowing that he did something horrible and not being able to put him away? We have to build a case. You know that. I don't have to tell you this."

"Of course, I know that." He shakes his head. "But what do I do with this? I wasn't expecting this at all. I was just walking around and all of a sudden, here it was."

"Do you think this would be enough to call the police?" I turn to Luke.

"There's not going to be enough for a warrant," Donald says. "What do we really have? You peeked into his window, saw a purse that may tie him to some far away case when it's probably her ex-husband who now has no alibi and a motive. Then we have me watching him and finding this little piece of disturbed ground."

"Which does look like a grave," I assure him.

"Maybe, but what judge is going to approve it? What judge is going to give them permission to search?" Donald snaps. "This looks like a grave, but we don't see a body. We don't have any incriminating evidence. The only way to do this is if you stumble upon it, you disturb the grave, you see what's in here. If we find a body or just a bone, which I think we might, then we have evidence for a warrant for everything else."

"Then it goes to court and he hires a good attorney and the attorney gets the original search warrant thrown out because it was a lie," I say. "We weren't covering our tracks. I told Captain Carville what you were working on. You talked to every department that would listen. We can't pretend that we found this by accident because if they find out everything else, he's never going to serve a single day in prison. He's going to be out there free to do whatever he wants."

Twenty minutes later, the issue is unresolved. We both dig in. Luke seems to side with me, and frankly, I believe Donald does as well. He just wants to be someone who's on the side of doing something rather than doing nothing. The possible grave remains in the grove and our ideas as to what to do next remain just as vague.

The hushed tones that we've spoken in somehow dissipate as the conversation grows more intense. We go in circles and get nowhere. Somewhere in the distance, I hear a thumping sound.

"Shhh," I say, interrupting Donald in the middle of his rant about the FBI and the legal system and the red tape that seems to be the bane of his existence. The thump continues.

"Wait, stop talking," I say louder this time. "I want to hear."

"What is it?"

"It's like someone's hitting something. Like a very loud muffled knock. Do you hear it?"

"Yes, I do." Luke perks up.

"Where is it coming from?"

"Underground."

We walk around, walking closer to the house. The cabin has an outdoor patio.

"Hey, over on the other side, on stilts. The sound seems to be coming from there."

It's not very tall so I have to kneel. When I do, the thumping sound gets louder. I move gardening equipment, rakes, and shovels out of the way. It is at that precise moment that I become aware of something concealed beneath a heap of bricks, which are arranged neatly atop a protective tarp. Initially, I thought it was laid on the ground, but when I lift it slightly, droplets of water pool and trickle down onto my hand and I see that it's actually a door.

There's a cellar here.

The thumping gets louder. Someone tries to say something but the sound is muffled and I can't understand a word.

"There's someone in there!" I yell.

Luke runs over and the two of us crawl on our stomachs, moving the rakes and shovels and an old bicycle further to the side. We have to move the bricks aside, but even then, shifting the bulky, waterlogged mass of plastic takes a while. That's when we see the two doors with a thick chain around the loops.

The pounding continues, growing more intense by the second, causing my anxiety to skyrocket. "We're here. We're police officers. We're going to help you!" I shout, hoping to reassure whoever is on the other side. Suddenly, I hear a faint, muffled voice, barely audible over the clamor. It sounds urgent and desperate, barely able to force out the word "Hurry." My heart races and my chest tightens. Time is of the essence, and we must act fast.

Luke, sensing the urgency in my tone, takes the lead, searching for any tools that could help us gain entry. His eyes light up as he spots a pair of heavy-duty deadbolt cutters, and he immediately begins to break the chain. I frantically clear away any other obstacles blocking the door's path.

Finally, with a loud snap, the chain breaks, and Luke wrenches the door open with all his might. As the dust settles, I catch a glimpse of a frail, barely clothed woman looking back at me with bewildered eyes.

Chapter 17

Her green eyes widen, round like saucers, filled with terror, flicker in the darkness. It takes me a moment to really see her, to comprehend the depth of her fear, and the profound relief that washes over her when she realizes that we are here to help. Her hands are bound in front of her, and a rag has been shoved into her mouth to silence her cries. She trembles as Luke pulls her out of the dark, cold cellar, his movements slow and cautious to prevent her from being hurt.

She is dressed in nothing but a white night-gown, which is stained with dirt and grime. Peering into the depths of the cellar, I am assaulted by the overwhelming stench of human excrement and decaying food. The floor is slick with standing water, and one wall appears to be collapsing in on itself.

With the gag removed from her mouth, I work to untie the ropes binding her hands, my hands fumbling with urgency. It's not until my task is complete that I finally find my voice, kneeling down to ask her name. Donald takes off his jacket, wrapping it around her.

"What happened? What are you doing here?"

"He's going to come back. He's going to kill you. We have to go," she says.

We had no idea when David Trincia would come back, but if he did, there was a very strong possibility that he would be armed. We, on the other hand, didn't come ready for a fight.

"We have a long way back to the cars." I turn to Donald. "We have to go through the trees if we don't want anyone to see us. We have to get her to a hospital. I have to call 911."

"My phone has a little bit of reception on that rock over there," Donald says. "Let me call them. We'll see how fast they can get out here."

We're suddenly regretting the fact that none of the three of us have a weapon. Donald should have brought his pistol but for some reason, he didn't, and I didn't want to travel with mine. I rarely bring it anywhere except for work. Donald hurries to get to that rock from which he called me and starts to talk to someone on the phone.

"The police are going to be here soon," I say.

"Tell me, what happened to you? Who are you?" But the girl just shakes and says nothing.

"How old are you?" I ask.

"Thirty-two," she says.

Calling her a girl isn't appropriate but the way she looks, I thought that she wasn't a day over eighteen. Her long brown hair is matted in places, oily in others, and wet. Her neck is covered in bruises, so is her body. She sits with her knees out and I can see how skinny her legs are, practically emaciated.

"Did he starve you?"

"Yes," she says. "He didn't give me food."

"What's your name?" I ask.

"Jodie. Jodie Schmidt," she says.

"How long have you been in there?"

"I don't know. I lost count a while ago. He took me and I didn't know who he was for a while. I thought he was going to kill me and then realized that it was going to be worse than that. He was going to keep me alive in there."

"How did he kidnap you exactly?" I ask.

"I was waiting at a bus stop." She speaks to me but doesn't make eye contact. "There was no one else around. It was nighttime. He came over and stood a little bit apart. We chatted for a moment, and then when I turned my head, he stuffed a rag in my mouth, and I passed out. I woke up here. I've been here ever since. It's been months."

"No one called for you?"

"I live alone," she says. "My parents died. I don't have many friends. I worked from my house. I'm sure the landlord thinks I just fell behind on the rent, took off, and left all my stuff but that's not what happened. You have to believe me."

"Of course, I believe you," I say.

"How did you find me?" she whispers and then hesitates. There's a sound out in the distance. She freezes at every little noise, like an abused animal.

"That's the police," I say. "Sirens. They're coming here."

A wave of relief washes over her.

"Okay, good, good," she says in a weak voice.

I glance over at Donald. He's practically giddy with excitement. I feel his anticipation.

"Was there anyone else here while you were here?" I ask. I wish I could give her something to drink. Her lips are parched, dry, and she coughs. Her voice is raspy, but I don't have anything. I drank the last bit of my water right before we came here.

"The paramedics and the police are going to have something for you, I promise. You're going to be fine."

She nods. I can feel the hesitant relief come over her. She relaxes a bit. Her shoulders are sloped down, not so hunched near her neck. I ask her again if there was anyone else.

"There was someone," she says. She meets my eyes for a moment and then looks away quickly.

"I heard them talking. I was in the cellar, but you could hear what was happening right up top at the same time. He tried to make nice with her like he did with me."

"What does that mean?" I ask.

"He wanted her to do things, but she wouldn't cooperate. She fought back, hard. I had convinced him that he didn't have to kill me, that I would do whatever he wanted, and I wouldn't run away. I had said it enough times that he started to believe me, and then I guess when he took the other girl, he thought maybe he could do the same thing with her."

"So, what happened to her?" I ask. Part of me already knows the answer.

"He killed her," she says in a matter-of-fact way that you would answer "fine" to a neighbor who asks, "How are you feeling today?"

"Do you know anything about her? Did you hear it happen?"

"Yes." She nods. "I did. I was here. I heard her screaming. I heard the thump. I knew that he had made her pass out with chloroform and then he killed her."

"Here?"

"Yes, in the cabin," she says.

If he had done it in the cabin, it means that there should be a plethora of evidence for all sorts of fibers and blood and DNA evidence.

"Do you know anything else about her?" I ask. "Her name, what she looked like, anything else."

"No. I don't know what happened to her, but I heard him calling her by her name."

"What was it?"

"Cora."

———

The arrival of the first cops on the scene offers me a sense of relief, knowing that the situation is now under control. I can only hope that David Trincia, if he decides to return, will see the many black and white police cars out front and think twice before approaching his cabin. Detective Clint Patterson arrives only twenty minutes later, after the initial patrol officers had already secured the area. I'm impressed by his promptness and attention to detail.

Detective Patterson is in his forties and he exudes a sense of meticulousness and neatness that gives off an engineer-like vibe. He holds a small recorder in his left hand, dictating his thoughts and notes with careful precision. It's clear to me that he plans to review the files later, either by himself or before sending them off to be transcribed. He comes off as a control freak, but I mean that in the best possible way - I tend to check and double-check my work as well.

He pursues this work more like an art rather than a science, which is exactly what it is. It's the details of a human condition, understanding the "whys" that help you get to the truth, rather than simply collecting DNA evidence and the like. It's believing in hunches despite all odds like Donald has. I haven't allowed myself to do that and I wonder how much time we lost and how much more suffering Jodie and others had gone through as a result.

We had conferred for a few moments right before the first patrol officer pulled up. I told Donald straight away that I'm not making up any stories.

"We weren't doing anything wrong. We heard her yelling and that's what happened."

"That's exactly what I was going to say." Donald nods.

They can't accuse us of any improper behavior here and so that's the exact story that we tell Detective Patterson. We've been following this guy, following hunches, that I was about to give up. The only reason we were out there in the first place was to look at the possible grave that Donald had found.

"Grave? What grave?" Clint asks, coming back to me long after our conversation is over. I take him up to the grove, the pine trees, and point to it.

"That's why Donald called us. That's why we were here. We're trying to figure out if there was enough evidence for a warrant, which neither of us thought there would be."

"And he did?"

"No, but it seemed like wishful thinking."

"Well, I got to tell you, finding a woman in a cellar kind of changes things a bit, doesn't it?" Patterson asks with a tight smile.

He's not trying to make light of things because he doesn't know how serious it is. The joke is kind of crude, probably improper, and if it were recorded and played on social media, it would look like he was mocking the victim, but he's not. Sometimes making jokes is the only way you can cope with the horrors that you experience, but I remind him that today is a good day. She wasn't dead, she was alive, safe, and that makes everything worth it.

Many long hours later, Clint invites us to the office for a more in-depth conversation. I want to pass, but I know that this is just the beginning of the investigation, and we need to be as helpful as possible.

"Come on, I'll treat you all to lunch," he says. "I just need to pick your brain and find out more about you guys."

Chapter 18

Lunch ends up being sandwiches from a little deli around the corner from the Fairview City Police Department eaten over our laps. While everybody else's desks are cluttered with paperwork without any rhyme, reason, or order, Detective Clint Patterson's workspace is pristine. There are all sorts of organizing bins, pens in little compartments, and even color coordination and style that looks like it's out of an IKEA showroom.

He doesn't have his own office, but his desk is by a large window that bathes everything in white light. We sit on chairs across from him and there's plenty of space to put down our food, which wouldn't be the case with any of the nearby officers. The desktop itself looks like it has been recently polished, pristine like the Apple Store. The FBI has been called in and we are introduced to special agent, Jennifer Rivers, a woman in her thirties with almond eyes, shoulder-length sandy hair, and a dry sense of humor that I find particularly appealing.

Thankfully, there's no posturing, no power struggle. She's there to help the department and to help us get to the bottom of what has happened. She listens carefully, takes notes in a black Moleskin leather notebook in small, neat print. She writes fast and the ink doesn't always have time to dry, smearing a little bit.

Chomping down on his Reuben sandwich, I can immediately sense a change in Donald's demeanor.

Finally, everyone is listening to his story, really listening, hanging on to every word, and believing the connections that he made, no matter how farfetched.

The first victim that he speaks of is a teenage runaway named Bree Zander. She was last seen in her room and there was footage of her riding a bus to Tacoma. She had started a job at Book Nook, which was owned by Frances Meeks, a woman in her fifties.

Swallowing another bite, Donald wipes his mouth and says, "Only Frances Meeks did not know that Bree Zander was Bree Zander. She only knew her by the name Danny Lofton. She was the one who had reported her missing when she didn't show up for work and frankly, she seemed more concerned about her whereabouts than her own parents."

"How did she go missing?" Jennifer asks.

"She was working the evening shift, in charge of closing. She was supposed to be there again the next afternoon, but she never showed up. Danny or Bree told Frances that she had moved to Tacoma with her parents, and she was going to the local school there, but that was not the case."

"How did she not know her real name?" Clint asks. "Wasn't there paperwork?"

"Apparently Frances was only going to work the store herself. She took pity on this girl who asked her for a job. She had no plans to hire anyone, so she didn't know how to set up payroll. She was paying her cash and Bree was obviously completely fine with that."

"Her parents never reported her missing?" Jennifer asks.

He nods.

"Yes, they did, but they reported her as a runaway, so it wasn't urgent, just something to keep an eye out for, as you know. She had worked at the store for over a month and because she went missing from a different jurisdiction, a connection was never made until much later. Once Frances started to make a big stink about her being missing, they checked out the place where she was supposedly living. The address that she gave Frances was bogus. She dropped her off there, so the police wanted to talk to this guy who lived in the apartment. He said that a girl named Danny Lofton was supposed to move in in a day or so. She had paid for a month for the room, but then she never showed up. He had no way of contacting her because her phone had stopped working, too."

"Did they investigate this guy?"

Donald nods. "Yes. He was one of the primary suspects, but he was in Portland visiting his dying mother in hospice at the time. There were records of him signing in and out and video footage of him being there. That's where the trail went cold. No one knew what happened to her afterward. She was later found drowned in a lake in Tacoma."

"Any other bruising or anything on her body?" Jennifer asks.

"Not really. I don't have access to the autopsy, but I didn't get that sense when I talked to the medical examiner. Her death was ruled as drowning but what was she doing there? Why was she there? Then why would Victor McFadden know about her whereabouts or her mysterious disappearance at all?"

The strands were loose, but they were becoming a little bit tighter. The case would still be difficult to make, given what we found at David Trincia's cabin.

We take a little break to get some coffee. Jennifer and I meet in front of the vending machine to cure our respective sweet teeth. She goes for a pack of Skittles, and I grab M&M's.

"This is quite a theory he's been working on."

"Yes. You don't even know the extent to which he went to get anyone to believe him."

"Like what?"

"Well, he got me to come up here to work the case when every other cop and agent rejected him. I guess you could almost call it bribery or blackmail."

"Why? He's got something on you?" Jennifer says, tossing her hair.

"I'll tell you some other time, I think I'll need a few drinks to get into that story."

"Got it. Rain check?"

"Definitely."

I ask her how long she's been an agent. She says two years.

"Wow. So, the FBI really believes that this is an important case to work, right?" I say with sarcasm.

"Seems like it." She smiles, taking it as joke.

"I'm sure they'll send more people once I do the work putting the reports together and convincing them that this is something real."

"Well, I'm glad to hear that, at least." I smile. Popping a handful of candy into my mouth, I enjoy the burst of chocolate and sugar rushing through my system. We talk a little bit about our lives and education, and I'm surprised how candidly she announces that she grew up in a trailer park up in North Seattle and that her father was a drunk and her mom became one as well.

"I just needed to get out of there. Ever since I was a kid, I knew I had to go to college otherwise I'd have no future. Somehow I managed to get into the University of Washington, even though I have to tell you my grades weren't that great. I really struggled with all the drama in my life. We moved from place to place, our lights and power would get shut off. It was a whole shit show, but my mom had me at sixteen. She had no way of making a living, she just, how do they say it? Relied on the kindness of strangers? In real life it was a little less romantic than in *A Streetcar Named Desire*." She smiles.

"How did you end up in the FBI?"

"I majored in English and psychology because I always wanted to just figure out why everything was so messed up in my life, how to deal with it, how to control my own emotions, that kind of thing. I was thinking of being a therapist, but then I found out about behavioral psychology, got interested in the dark side, so to speak, and frankly, I wanted a steady job, but I wanted it to be exciting. The FBI was at the career fair my senior year. I was doing my thesis on criminology and psychology, and they told me about the behavioral psychology unit out there and all the things that I could do. It was going to be steady work, too, government job with a pension, stability that I never had. It was a dream."

"How is it for you now?"

"I love it. I mean, there are aspects of the job that I don't particularly like, certain colleagues of course, but in general, it's been amazing. Just waking up every day and knowing that I'm doing something that's good for the country, is good for people, finding bad guys, putting them away, so when I saw this case come up and no one was really that interested, I just jumped on it. I'm not scared of the dark side of people. Maybe I should be, but I've seen a lot and I'm more interested in what makes them tick, you know?"

"Yes, I do. I like that," I say. "Sorry, I don't mean to be rude, but you said you've only been working for two years?"

She nods. "Yes."

"I know there was training and everything, but did you work somewhere else before this?"

"It wasn't as linear a path as I'd wanted. I got my master's degree, started my PhD, then dropped out. I hate to admit it, the exams were brutal, and school was hard for me. I don't know why I'm telling you all this stuff, but we just seem to have a little bit of a connection."

"No, I love it."

I did. I shared my own story, my own convoluted way that I got to the LAPD, and she smiled at all the different ways that we connect and finally, I tell her about my father.

"He was really the impetus. I thought that going there, I would find out what had happened, and then I found out that it was suicide," I say.

It feels comfortable talking to her. There's something honest about her that is difficult to pinpoint. Perhaps like a good therapist, she listens. She allows you to open up and feel comfortable with things that you never told anyone because there's no reason to be embarrassed by the things that happened to you. They were only opportunities to learn more about yourself and the people around you.

"I guess you found out what you wanted, right?" she asks.

"Kind of," I admit. "But then I got this letter from Donald calling me up here. He told me there was more to the story, that he was forced to commit suicide. That it was actually murder. That's how he got me to come up here. That's how he got me to listen to him, to this case. He knew something with the intercepted communications. What will I do with that now? I guess it's up to me."

"Oh, wow. That's rough. All these years later," she says. "I'm sorry."

When she touches my arm, I feel a wave of emotion come over me. A tear almost escapes, but I take a few deep breaths and calm myself down.

"I told you I'd need a drink before I talked about that." I smile and pop a red M&M in my mouth. "We better get back, there's a lot more to the story you haven't heard yet."

Chapter 19

As soon as we get back, Donald opens up the second half of his sandwich, takes a bite, chews, and then jumps into the story about the second victim: twenty-five-year-old Frieda Wolfe. He's usually pretty good about not talking with his mouth full, but on this occasion, it's like he can't help himself.

Jennifer and Clint listen intently, hanging on every word, occasionally pausing to take sips of coffee, munch on a few more Skittles (in Jennifer's case), or fiddle with his pen (in Clint's case).

"The first people to grow concerned about Frieda," Donald says, "were her students. She didn't show up to teach her assigned math classes. They called her, told the department head, and the secretary there called the school police to go check on her. Since she lived off campus in a studio and she lived alone, it was easy for her to get lost. They estimate that she had been gone maybe ten days before anyone really started looking."

"What happened to her?" Jennifer asks.

"She was found shot in the back of her head, execution-style, in a park about fifty miles away from her apartment. It was a remote area. There were no bullet casings, and they're not sure that she was even killed there. Probably just dumped."

"Those are the hardest cases," Jennifer says. "When the body's transported, you have two crime scenes and you have to connect them somehow. Well, in this case, you just have one. We have no idea where he did it or if he left any evidence behind."

I think back to the cabin, if all of them had been killed right there, there must be some evidence of that. As we speak, CSI is probably going through the cabin. Everything had been marked off. Clint won't be able to stay for long. He has an actual crime scene to oversee. Lunch hasn't even been forty-five minutes, but we all know that he has to get back.

"Tell me about the last one," he says, looking at his smartwatch.

"It was a little boy, six, named Langley Daniels. He was taken from a park while the babysitter was talking with some friends that she ran into. He was found later that night with his neck sliced."

A shiver runs up my spine. I had heard the story before, of course, but the thought of a little boy being killed by a merciless murderer makes me want to commit any number of atrocities against that guy, bring him back from the dead, and do it all over again at least.

"I have to get back now," Clint says. "Thanks for all the info. I'd invite you to the cabin, but the rain is picking up and we can't have anyone coming in and out observing the crime scene at all."

"Of course." I nod.

"I'll be right there," Jennifer says.

"Take your time."

The four of us remain. Luke has been quiet this whole time, almost lost in his own thoughts. Jennifer looks excited. She had written down about three pages of notes from what Donald had said. From the expression on his face, I can tell that Donald is practically overcome with glee that someone finally believes him, that he is not a crazy old man with insane ideas. He had told them about Victor McFadden and how he had found out about these three cases being connected in the first place, and I saw Jennifer take careful notes.

"We'll be interviewing him, of course," she says. Donald shrugs.

"I'm sure he'd be happy to talk to someone. He talked to Kaitlyn."

"Oh, he did?"

"Yes." I nod. "I took notes of our meeting. I can send them over, but it was pretty much what Donald said. He's very earnest. He seems to just want to help but I had some doubts as you can imagine."

"Of course, until the cabin." Jennifer smiles.

"Yes, the cabin and the woman."

I bite the inside of my lip wondering how we got so lucky as to be there and rescue her. I want to speak to her again but she's in the hospital recovering, and Clint should be the first one to interview her. Nothing she would say to me would be in any sort of official capacity. I know that I have to step back and let the people with actual jurisdiction take care of this. But still, when Jennifer packs up her notebook and her fountain pen and tosses them into her elegant leather tote bag, I know that I'll probably head over to the hospital just to see how she's doing. Maybe she'll talk to me, maybe she won't, but I'll have to try.

"How long are you in town?" Jennifer asks.

"That's been kind of up in the air." I smile.

"Well, a few more days, right?"

"Looks like it."

I look at Luke and he gives an approving nod.

"Let's meet up and grab a drink sometime,

both of you," she says, adding Luke as a little bit of an afterthought.

I know that he probably didn't take that as an insult, and that's not how she meant it.

"Of course." I smile. "Hey, do you happen to know what hospital they took Jodie Schmidt to?" I ask just as she's about to walk away.

Chapter 20

The Fairview Valley Community Hospital is small with low-lying ceilings and '70s architecture. Anyone over 6'4" would practically have to duck to get through the hallways but the nursing staff is friendly enough and accommodating, showing me where I can find her, leading me through the hallways to her room.

I'm pleased to see that a patrol officer has been stationed outside and they check both mine and Luke's IDs to make sure that we're not some imposters just in case David Trincia tries to look for her.

The hospital room smells like Twizzlers and lilacs. Jodie is chomping on one long red string when I come in and smiles broadly as soon as she sees me. Luke decided to stay in the hallway just to not overwhelm her with too many people at once.

"Hey, how are you? Just checking in."

"I'm good. Thanks for coming."

"Oh, I wasn't sure if you'd want to see me."

"No, of course, I do." She smiles. "They put me in here and said that I had to stay for a couple of days, but there's nothing really wrong with me."

It's kind of an odd statement from a girl who was found in a cellar, and whose whole body is covered in bruises. I can see where she's coming from, though. Wearing a warm sweater with a blanket tucked all around her and big fluffy socks on her feet sticking out from underneath, she somehow looks as happy as a clam being here. Of course she is, given where she has spent the last few months.

"Did anyone come to talk to you?" I ask.

"Not really. One of the officers said that detectives are going to come back, but that one who was there, Detective Patterson, hasn't come yet."

"Yes, he's still at the scene," I say. "They're going to be looking at the cabin and collecting evidence."

"Did he send you?"

"No, I'm not officially on the case, I'm just helping out, you could say, but I was thinking that maybe you'd be here alone, and maybe you'd want some company. But if you don't, if you just want to watch TV and eat Twizzlers, let me know. I'll get out of your hair."

"No, please don't. I've been alone way too long, it's nice to see a friendly face. You want one?" She offers a string and I accept.

"I got two more packets. The nurses are really taking care of me."

"Good. I'm glad to hear that," I say. "There's an officer right outside, so you don't have to worry about anyone else getting in here."

"No, I'm not."

"I'm not just talking about David. I'm talking about the news people, reporters, they're probably going to come around soon."

"Yes, I guess they will."

"How do you feel about talking to them?"

"Actually, I don't know. Okay, I guess. I kind of want people to know, you know." She tilts her head, looking suddenly very small and frail, but incredibly strong.

"I can't believe I used to weigh 170 pounds. I haven't stepped on the scale, but my wrists are all bones," she says. "I was dieting nonstop before it happened. I guess it just takes a couple of months of not eating, huh?"

She forces a smile. I give her one back.

I don't want to jump into the case right away.

Instead, I ask her about her life before, but she shakes her head.

"No, I don't want to talk about that right now," she says. "Can you just stay here and we can watch some TV?"

"Of course."

She flips through the channels landing on MTV and *Teen Mom*.

"I used to love this show," she says. "I'd have these marathons all day long. I'd record them and just binge-watch late into the night."

We sit quietly watching as a girl argues with the father of her child about child support. She turns down the volume about five minutes later and turns to look at me.

"It's hard to zone out now. It's like I can't just watch the show anymore and enjoy it. I keep getting these flashbacks of what happened."

"I'm really sorry. I'm not a therapist, but it's probably going to be a good idea for you to talk to one. I'm sure you have a lot of post-traumatic stress and that's what the flashbacks are."

"Yes, probably. It's like I can't get that cabin out of my mind. I can't get his eyes...do you know where he went? David Trincia? Is that his name?" she asks.

"He didn't tell you his name?"

"No." She shakes her head.

"He told me to call him Jones, Brother Jones."

"Brother Jones?"

"He was religious but in kind of an odd way. He had this altar in the cabin and he would collect twigs and animal bones, put them there with the rocks and some crystals. This altar was on top of his dresser. He would close his eyes and pray for long periods of time, standing there in this trance."

I stop chewing, letting the fragments of the Twizzler just stay on top of my tongue as I stare at her.

"He wanted me to call him Brother Jones when he first took me, and then just Jones when I guess he got more comfortable."

"Where were you when he prayed like that?" I ask.

"Tied up next to the stove. That's what he liked to do. The stove was really hot, so you couldn't press yourself against it. It was really uncomfortable. My arms were behind me and so were my legs. Sometimes, he let my legs go free and I could just sit there but I couldn't get out. The knots were tight and he was really meticulous. He said I was the first person that he had let go, but he had to pray to make it better."

"He was very religious then?"

"Yes."

"Did he talk about God all the time?"

"Actually, no, but he said that he did what he

did because God sent this demon after him and then he had to make it better. The only way he made him go away was through sacrifice."

"Why did he keep you alive?" I ask.

"I begged him to, and he said he would try, and he would do his best, but only if I behaved. I was looking for a way out, but I couldn't see a good one."

"When would he put you in the cellar?" I ask.

"Whenever he left. There were also long periods of time when he was home and I still had to stay there. I was usually tied up to a post, but this time it was a little loose. I guess he wasn't as careful as he usually was, and I was able to untie that part, but I couldn't open the padlock. That's when I heard you guys talking. There were multiple people, and no one seemed distressed, it's like you were arguing and I just knew I had to get myself free to pound on the door. I just had to tell someone that I was there, but part of the time I wasn't even sure I heard what I thought I heard. I was terrified it was him, but I did it anyway because it felt like my only chance."

"You were very brave to do that. I know that required a lot of courage, but I'm so glad that you did, so glad that you heard us. We were talking about a grave out back by the grove. I don't know if you were outside the cabin that much, but there's a disturbed piece of land that Donald thought might be the grave of a little kid, but we couldn't disturb it. If we found the body and we didn't have a warrant to be there, it wouldn't be admissible, we'd have nothing, so we were standing there arguing about what to do."

"How did you know about the cabin?"

"Donald has suspected him for a while now." I tell her the whole story, and she listens quietly, nodding her head.

"I don't know what's in the grave, if it's a grave," she says at the end. "He always said how he never shit where he ate. He was proud of that fact. The way he talked about it made me think that he always put the bodies somewhere far away, other towns, cities so the connections couldn't be made."

"Yes, I'm getting that sense," I say.

"I'm really surprised that you guys found the cabin since you were just following him at noon and stuck around and actually looked," she says, opening another pack of Twizzlers. "I thought it would be because that little boy got away. I thought maybe he told his parents, and they told the police or something like that."

I blink once, twice.

"What little boy?" I ask after a moment.

Chapter 21

I stop chewing and a little bit of Twizzler remains on the tip of my tongue, suddenly feeling like a foreign object. It has lost the sweetness of its sugary coating. It feels more like rubber than anything else. The phrase "little boy" lingers and time seems to slow down. Jodie smiles and even laughs feverishly opening another bag and taking a generous bite. She hasn't noticed that I have entered some trance, uncertain as to when I will regain my ability to speak.

"Are you okay?" she finally asks.

"What little boy?"

"What?"

"You said that you thought that we came because of a little boy, that maybe he went to his parents and told them about this and that's why we came," I repeat her words verbatim to the best of my ability.

The only little boy that I know of is Langley Daniels, whose body was found after he had disappeared from the playground.

"Had someone gotten away?" I ask.

"Well, yes, but he was never really taken. He just showed up there one time. It was so odd. He had ridden his bike and I thought maybe he was lost. Jones saw him from the window. He went out onto the porch to talk to him, but the boy got spooked and he took off. I could see from the window that there was something wrong with his tire, but he forced it anyway and Jones didn't go after him. You have no idea how lucky he got. He probably wouldn't be here if he had knocked on the door and asked for help."

"What did he look like?"

"Shaggy hair, longer sides, white, rosy cheeks, looked about five or six. I remember after that night, I just kept praying that he went home and told his parents about the cabin. Maybe they'd come by, but as the weeks passed, I realized that he didn't see anything suspicious. We were just people in a cabin. Jones just came out onto the porch and yelled for him to stop. Even if he had told someone, what would he have said? Nothing of consequence."

She looks sad and I am perplexed more than

anything. I finally manage to swallow the little bit of rubbery Twizzler in my mouth, excuse myself, and make a phone call.

Later that day, scouring the missing persons reports with Clint, we discover that there's no information about any little boy matching that description that was filed in the vicinity who was reported missing.

"How could that be?" I ask.

"We checked within a five-mile radius, which would be already way too far for a boy to get to on his bike. Where did he come from? She could be mistaken."

"No, I didn't get that sense."

Clint shakes his head as well. "Me neither."

"What could have happened?"

"Perhaps the parents or guardians didn't report him missing."

"Yes, it is a possibility, but he's so young. What was he doing out for so long? It would've taken him, I don't know, maybe half an hour at least to go down that road. They didn't notice that he was gone?"

"Not everyone's paying attention so closely, unfortunately," Clint says. "Maybe he snuck out. Family's doing something else, busy with other kids. Never noticed that he was gone."

"What do you suppose happened?"

"Maybe he just came back, never said a word

to anyone. Would you? If you snuck out of the house and a scary thing happened to you and you knew that you were doing something wrong, even at that age, would you tell an adult who you don't necessarily trust, maybe someone who might hit you or yell at you for leaving in the first place?"

C lint goes back to talk to Jodie, and I leave the hospital to get some fresh air. Luckily, it's not raining, and the sun is even peeking out through the clouds. That little boy is either the luckiest little guy ever or a fiction. I don't want to doubt her. She had showed me no reason why I should, but doubts still creep in.

What would be the motive? Why make something like that up? I don't know the answer to that any more than I know the answer to any of the questions that are suddenly popping into my mind.

I'm incredibly thankful that we found her, that she's alive, and who knows what else we can find in the cabin? The scene is still being processed, but my doubts don't change the fact that I want to find him. Where could he have come from?

I pull up Google Maps and zoom in on the nearby houses. Sometimes, from the satellite you can see stuff in the yards, like bikes. You probably couldn't tell the color, of course, and the satellite image could be from a long time ago, but I might get lucky and see if there are kids in a particular house. Kids leave their bikes all over the place. They wouldn't necessarily put it inside, especially if it's wet and covered in mud.

I check the nearby houses closest to the cabin. That's most likely where he came from, but I see nothing other than debris, random knickknacks and junk; no evidence of any of them having children. No swing sets, no trampolines.

Then about a mile out, there's a two-story building that looks like a motel. I click on it and see that it's an apartment building with ten units in total. There is a swing set in the back, and that means that there are probably kids who live there or have lived there. I see no bikes on the satellite, but it is worth talking to someone there. It's nearing five o'clock at night, dinner time. If I do it today, this is the best time. Parents will be home and kids will still be awake.

For a moment I debate whether to ask for Clint's permission, but I'm not officially with the department. I'm not working this case in any law enforcement capacity, and I worry that he might say no. Instead of asking permission, I'll ask for forgiveness.

I text Luke that I have an idea and to meet me outside. I decide to leave Donald buried in his computer in the waiting room, chomping down on a burger. Three people showing up, including two FBI agents, might be too daunting and cause people to clam up. I tell Luke my idea, and though he tries to dissuade me, he doesn't try hard.

"It's probably best if you talk to them alone," he says.

Chapter 22

On the short drive, we talk about the case and how exciting and rewarding it was to find Jodie. You don't get moments like that often, but when you do, you cherish them.

"Are you sure that you still want to quit this line of work even after finding her?" I ask.

"Well, I'm not going to say that it doesn't feel good to have this resolution." Luke smiles. "But it's hard. Most of the time, it's just missing people, dead bodies, unsolved cases. I think you're much better with living the unknown, the uncertainty, than I am. I want things to make sense."

"Yes, I get that. I'll support you, whatever you want to do," I say.

"Even if it means staying home and taking care of the kids?"

"Of course. Kids? Wait a second. We never talked about *multiple* kids."

"Come on, you can't just have one?"

"Of course, you can," I say. "I'm not even entirely sold on one. It's really scary."

"I know," he says. "It is going to be fun, though. It means a lot of sleepless nights, and all that, but afterward when they're a little older, four, five, six, it'll be a blast."

When he mentions that age, my heart sinks. David Trincia was likely responsible for the death of one six-year-old that we know of.

Who knows how many others? This kid that we were looking for, who might have been a witness to him being inside that cabin, who might have seen him with Jodie, was likely in that age range as well. We both don't say anything for a moment, which then turns into a long pause. I have no doubt that we're both thinking about the same thing.

The child that we're looking for had been incredibly lucky, but now his life is going to be turned around. If he did see David Trincia in that cabin, he's one of our primary eyewitnesses. He could place him at the scene. If he doesn't recognize him, when this case goes to trial, Trincia's lawyers would also try to put him up on the stand to prove that no, he wasn't there after all.

We park in front of the weathered red brick

apartment building. I feel nauseated, part of me hoping this boy isn't there after all.

"What if we don't look for him?" I ask Luke. "What if we can't find him?"

"I'm sure they're going to be canvassing this place anyway. Clint knows about this boy, and he's an eyewitness."

"I shouldn't have told him right away. Seemed like such a break, but if he's five or six, that's way too much to deal with, but he could have seen something."

"The DNA is going to prove whether he was there one way or another, unless Trincia scrubbed that cabin, and he might have."

I shake my head no. "I doubt that. That was his safe place. That's where he took people. That's where he kept Jodie for so long. I don't think that he would have been as meticulous about it as he would have been if it were some other place."

"His parents never reported him missing," I add. "That means that they had no idea that he was missing or didn't want anyone to know that he had disappeared."

"We won't know anything until we actually talk to him," Luke says.

I force myself out of the car and slam the door shut. No one answers the first two doors we knock on and I let out a sigh of relief. The woman who opens the third one is pleasant, elderly, with her hair in curlers and wearing a bathrobe. A little dog yaps. She tries to quiet her down, eventually just closing the door behind her and stepping onto the landing. No, she doesn't have a little boy living with her, but there's one who lives upstairs in the apartment on the corner. There are teenagers above her head, and she complains about them playing loud music at night. There are also twin girls, who are about ten, who live two doors down.

This woman seems to know everything about everyone in the building. We head straight to the apartment that she points to. It takes a while for someone to come to the door, but there are corresponding numbers in the parking lot to the parking spaces, to the address and we know that at least someone must be home. There's an old Toyota Corolla parked under Apartment 8.

The man who answers is clearly intoxicated. He's wearing boxer shorts and pulls on a stained white t-shirt to cover up his substantial beer belly. He looks to be in his thirties, but out of shape and with red cheeks and a bulbous nose, sure tell signs of progressed alcoholism.

"Who are you?" he asks.

I decide against using my title quite yet, keeping it in the back pocket, and introduce myself simply as Kaitlyn Carr here to ask a few questions about his son.

"Why? What did he do? That little son of a bitch," he snaps.

He opens the door slightly, looking back at the living room, which is covered in toys, papers, magazines, and some other debris. A boy sits on the couch practically being eaten by the cushions. The couch is large, overstuffed, and overwhelmed with clothes and toys.

"Hey, Nicky. These people are asking about you. Come here," the father snaps.

The boy freezes. He looks at us with bewildered eyes.

He walks up slowly looking down at the floor, hanging his shoulders and his head. He has shaggy hair, white, almost translucent skin.

"He didn't do anything wrong. He just might have seen something and we wanted to ask him a few questions. Would you mind?"

"Sure. Go ahead," he snaps and doesn't make a move to leave.

"Do you have a bike, Nicky?" I ask in the nicest voice possible.

"Yeah. Mm-hmm," he mumbles.

"Say yes." The man smacks him on his back and the boy's eyes fill with fear.

"Do you ever take it riding around the neighborhood and into the woods?"

"He's not supposed to go out there," the dad growls.

"Yes, but sometimes we all do things we're not supposed to, right? I remember I used to when I was little. Have you ever taken it out into the woods? I promise you won't get in trouble."

I look up at the dad, glaring at him.

"This is very important that you tell me the truth."

"Yes," he mumbles.

"Did you ever see a cabin? This was probably a couple of weeks ago."

"I rode once for a while," he said, "and I got lost."

"What? When was this?" His dad interrupts.

"Sir, look," Luke says. "There's something that happened at that cabin, and we really need to hear the truth from your son about what he saw. He might have been an eyewitness. Do you understand?"

"What are you talking about?" the dad asks. "Eyewitness to what?"

"I can't say in front of your son, but if you follow me out to the landing out there, we can have a chat."

Chapter 23

Luke pulls him away and I let out a sigh of relief that he ended up coming with me after all. I return to Nicky, who doesn't seem to trust me any more than he did earlier. I crouch down instead of leaning over him so that we're face-to-face. I tell him that it's very important that he tells me the truth and ask him if he knows the difference between truth and a lie. He nods yes and replies that his teacher told him. Then I ask the question again. I promise him that he won't be in trouble no matter the answer. He hesitates, but says nothing.

"Your parents probably don't know, right?" I ask. "They don't know that you've gone there because you're not supposed to." He nods. "The thing is that you might have seen something. You might have seen someone there, and I just want to find out from you what exactly happened."

"I rode my bike for a while," he starts slowly. "My parents were fighting a lot. They usually fight a lot. They didn't notice that I left. I'm not supposed to go in the woods, but it's boring on the roads and there are too many cars. One car nearly hit me once, so I went into the woods. I got lost. My tire got a hole in it, so it wasn't working so well. I saw a cabin out far away. I thought I would ask them for help."

"What happened? What kind of cabin was this?"

"Just wood. It was all by itself."

I realize that he must have come from the forest angle. That way, he wouldn't have seen the other houses nearby. "I came up to it, and then there was a light on inside. There was a woman there and a man," he says.

"Okay, were you going to knock on the door?"

"Yes, but then the door opened, and the man came out."

"What happened then?" My heart jumps into the back of my throat.

"I could see this green light around him, like he was bad. Like in cartoons, when someone is a ghost, they put that green light around them. He said something to me, but I turned around and I got on my bike and ran away as fast as I could. I thought that he would call my parents but I just knew he was a bad guy, and I didn't want to talk to him."

"Good, good," I say. "That was a very good thing that you did. You made a very good choice."

He smiles.

"You know what, you don't have to talk to any adults you don't feel good about. If you feel like something is wrong and he is a bad guy, you trust that. You follow your gut. Okay? You can't worry about hurting adults' feelings, you need to think about yourself."

He smiles and takes a step forward and gives me a hug. I suddenly get choked up and I feel like I'm about to cry. I take a few deep breaths to keep the tears at bay. He has no idea how close he came to being one of David Trincia's victims, and yet here was this unquantifiable, almost magical reason why he's still here. He felt like that guy was no good, and he followed his instincts and left.

We all have those worries, and sometimes, they're prejudices and they're wrong, but other times, they're spot on. The thing about growing up is learning the difference.

"Can I ask you something else?"

He nods.

"Did you see his face, what he looked like?"

"No, not really. There was light coming from behind him so I couldn't see his face. Just lots of shadows, it was all black. He had short hair. He was an adult like my dad," he adds.

"Okay, good, good."

I tell him to expect the police. "The good guys are going to come and ask you more questions about this. I want you to tell them what you told me, okay? You might have to tell your story a few times to different people, but it's very important."

"Is it because that guy's a very bad guy?"

"That's what we're trying to find out, but it looks like it." I nod.

⸻

The boy promises that he will tell the truth and tell the same story that he tells me to Clint and the others. I wonder how many times I ask him to repeat the story, how long it will be before he starts to second-guess himself, maybe elaborate, maybe take away bits and parts of it. We all do that when we tell stories over and over again, and he's only six years old. To expect him to be any different would be foolish.

I have also made a promise to him that I know I can't keep. The fear of his father in his eyes tells me a lot. This is not a man that is afraid to yell at his son, slap him, raise his hand, perhaps even use the belt on more than one occasion. He flinches when his father touches him, and his father makes no qualms about being rather aggressive, even in front of me, a stranger and a law enforcement officer. I have promised him that nothing will happen, and my only hope is that Luke has instilled a bit of fear into the father to make him keep his hands off his son, and hopefully not punish him for disappearing that night.

Now it makes perfect sense why no one reports him missing. It is likely that the father is drunk, passed out on the couch, or perhaps he and the mom are fighting that night, and the boy has escaped for some time away just like he says. Neither parent pays much attention and he is likely not gone so long that they would notice.

I hate the fact that we have brought him into this case. I hate that he is the only witness, other than Jodie, but I am thankful for the fact that he thinks that he sees a bad guy and he follows his gut and he is alive as a result.

Where to go from here is unclear. Finger-prints, DNA evidence, all the evidence from the crime scene will take a while to come back even if they're expedited and processed as quickly as possible. A week is optimistic, it will be a month if not more, depending on the resources of the county.

I start looking into flights and I know that I need to go back home. Hours of work to make up, besides, I'm not needed here anymore. Donald knows this, too; he says as much. Besides, he's so busy with his head buried in this investigation that I doubt he'd miss us much.

Still, my thoughts return to the little boy, and how your whole life can change in an instant. What if he makes a different decision? If he doesn't leave the apartment at all, he wouldn't be a witness, but if he doesn't listen to his gut, he wouldn't be here at all.

The same turn of luck happens to my sister. Only she isn't so lucky at first, and then she is. It's almost like she can read my mind because suddenly, she sends me a text saying, "Hey, why don't you come home?"

Chapter 24

On the flight back, Luke and I keep to ourselves. It's awkward to talk about anything in particular, being crammed into those little seats with barely space for your feet. I try to zone out with an audiobook, but I'm sitting in the middle, and the guy in the window seat has shamelessly taken over my armrest. I could push him, of course, but that would require me to actually touch him, something that I really don't want to do.

When the flight attendant comes around I ask for pretzels instead of crackers and for a hot tea. I briefly consider getting a drink, an actual one, but I think that being 30,000 feet up in the air is just going to make me feel even more frustrated, annoyed by everything. Instead, I opt to zone out as best I can.

My thoughts return to the call that I got from

Violet earlier this morning. She was excited to not just speak to me, but to see me. This is the most progress we've made since the kidnapping.

Prior to this, we've only texted a few times and she was always the first one to go. It's like talking to me was a reminder of what had happened. I know better than to think that she's ungrateful. I was the one who found and saved her. I was also the one who had seen her in that space. I was the one who had seen her in that vulnerable state.

She probably didn't want to be reminded of that when she was trying to move on with her life. No matter how much it hurt me, I got it. I knew that she would come around, and here she was, texting, calling. The conversation this morning came out of the blue. I was still packing but I stopped because I couldn't let this go, I couldn't push her away at this moment when she was reaching out. She told me about how much Mom was watching her every move and how she felt like she was partly in prison. I asked her about her online school. She said she liked it a lot since she could get far ahead of her work and then forget about it for weeks at a time.

"You know, that's not how it's supposed to be done," I joke. She had always been precocious.

I know that Mom is probably obsessing over when she'll start in person again. I know because she has called me plenty of times asking me to pester Violet about going back to school, but I don't want to put any undue pressure on her. I don't bother asking about her future plans. For now, enjoying the present is enough.

"I started seeing this therapist," Violet says. "Mom insisted that I go, of course, I really didn't want to, but then I did it as a favor to her and she's actually great. She's in her late twenties. I feel like she's actually met a teenager before. She can actually talk to me about things that are important, like she's not from outer space."

I chuckle. "I get it."

"Anyway, I told her about you and how close we were, I wanted to live with you. She thought it'd be a good idea for me to reach out to call you and see you again."

"Oh, of course, I would love that."

"But you're in Seattle, right?"

"Actually, my flight back is today. I still have a few more days off so I can come see you," I say.

I can feel her grinning on the other end.

"I was thinking of some things we can do that would be fun," Violet says. "Maybe go to the Red Barn and go bowling like we used to."

"I'd like that." I nod. "I'd like that very much."

We used to go there every Thursday night. We even joined the league. She was very good. Me, not so much. I would try to go anytime I was home, but the league was a weekly thing, and it was hard for me to drive up two hours and make time for that every single week.

"Do you want to go to the library, too?" she asks.

"Of course, it's another one of our favorites."

When she was younger, I would take her every Friday after school since I was typically off Thursday through Sunday. I would sometimes come up to visit her, and Mom of course. I chuckle at the afterthought. After school we'd spend hours with our heads buried in the stacks finding a list of new things to read. When she was little, our interests varied.

She was obsessed with *Ramona and Beezus* and I loved anything by Karin Slaughter but then our interests just started to converge. Once she got a little older, we read Virginia Woolf and *Catcher in the Rye* and all sorts of other books, many probably deemed inappropriate for young growing minds. She had only turned fourteen. It was nice talking to her this morning and seeing glimpses of her personality that were coming back.

When she first survived that horrendous ordeal, I wasn't sure that she would ever come out of that half comatose state. I thought maybe she would turn to drugs or worse and try to deal with it by escaping into some kind of self-destructive behavior.

"I'm glad the therapist is working out and you have someone to talk to. It's really important."

"I always had someone to talk to," Violet says. "You. I just didn't reach out when I should have."

"I really appreciate that, honey, but I'm not a psychologist. You can always talk to me about anything, but I won't always have the right answers."

"Well, I'm glad I have both of you then and maybe Mom can start butting out of my business."

"She will at some point. I'll try to talk to her," I say.

I was always acting as a mediator between the two of them. Now that she is back, it occurred to me that she still has a good four years of living under Mom's roof. I know Mom has become a little bit more understanding about her place in the world and probably a little bit grateful that she got her daughter back despite all the odds. But she is still my mom; nosy, overbearing, difficult, stubborn, and unwavering. She has been that way since I was a kid. It's partly what drove me away from home. If it weren't for Violet, I doubt that my visits would occur more than twice a year.

It is time to put our tray tables up, seats back into their upright position, and get ready for landing. I let out a sigh of relief. The flight wasn't long, but it was uncomfortable, and I can't wait to get back.

Chapter 25

Just as our plane is landing, Luke and I start talking about the future.

"In a hypothetical sort of scenario, where would be the ideal place to get married?" he asks.

I haven't given the ceremony any thought whatsoever, but he apparently has.

"Where would you like it to be? In a big banquet hall, country club, a church, on the beach, in the mountains, some other exotic destination?"

"Hmm, exotic destination sounds fun," I say, "But asking everyone to come out and make a whole trip of it sounds a little bit daunting. It would also be nice to go on a honeymoon ourselves without the family being there."

He laughs.

"Yes, I was thinking along those same lines. We should go on a honeymoon."

"Where do you think?" I ask.

"Definitely a beach."

"But where? Somewhere warm?" I add. "They do have beaches in the UK, you know."

"Yeah, I don't think so. No cold sandy beaches for me."

"But how about the South Pacific, Bora Bora?"

"That sounds expensive," I say, tilting my head.

"It is, but how often do you get married?"

"Well, some people get married like three times, so I really have to save my pennies here."

He shoves me a little, laughing at my joke.

"How about a destination wedding within Southern California?" he asks. "We've got the beach option; we've got the mountains in the summertime option by the lake. Then, of course, there's wine country in Temecula, and the desert, Palm Springs."

"Those all sound awesome," I say.

"Man, we really live in a beautiful place."

"Yes, lots of options."

"Not sure we can afford that many of them, though, but if we agree to something, we can start saving."

I want to bring up the fact that money might

be hard to come by, especially if he quits his cushy job for the federal government, but I opt against it.

"I wouldn't want to do anything very big," I say after a long pause, just as the wheels touch down on the ground. "Probably just close family and friends. Your family's quite big, but let's not be inviting the neighbors and the whole world."

"I'm with you on that."

"What about you?" I ask. "Beach, mountain lake, wine country, or the desert, which do you opt for?"

"The beach is quite beautiful and so are the mountains," he says, "But the last time we went to the mountains put me off of it for a while."

I smile knowing that he's referencing the burns and the murder that happened up there as well as my sister's disappearance.

"For me, it would have to be between wine country and the desert. Have you been to Palm Springs, those breathtaking mountains? It goes from almost sea level up to-- what is it? 10,000 feet, bright blue skies, seventy-five degrees in January. They have a lot of nice hotels there that aren't that expensive. With those views and the big pools upfront."

"That sounds great," I say, taking his hand as we make our way toward baggage claim.

"I'm not a big fan of wine, anyway. Let's do the desert."

He smiles and gives me a squeeze.

"Okay. I'm going to hold you to it. I'm not planning this thing myself," he says.

"No, of course not. We'll do it together. It's a lot of work and neither of us have planned a wedding before, so who the heck knows what we're getting into?"

"I love you, Kaitlyn."

He reaches down and kisses me softly on the lips. I kiss him back, losing all sense of time and place for a moment. We lock lips a little bit too long. When we pull away, I see the stares of onlookers, and then I reach over and kiss him again.

"I love you, too," I mumble.

———

Talking about wedding plans leaves me a little perplexed, not so much because I'm not excited. I am. Just, it feels strange to be engaged. Unlike other girls, I've never dreamed of getting married. I never gave it any thought whatsoever. I've had relationships and they just sort of ran their course without ever getting to this point. I wouldn't say that I've been a commitment phobe, but I guess looking back it was something like that.

Now, being with Luke, everything is different. It's like life finally makes sense, even though perhaps I don't deserve it. Things have fallen into place. I've prioritized our time together and I'm conscious of the fact that when I work too many days in a row, I really need to make time for him. He has done the same, and it feels good to have a partner day-to-day, have someone to call, have someone to be with, and even make long-term plans with.

It's more than that. I'm in love with him. I love everything about him, but mostly I love that being with him is not a chore. It's not work. It's not a time commitment that I don't want to make. I look forward to dinners, weekends, and days off. Unlike in the past, there have always been things that have annoyed me about my previous boyfriends, things that I thought I would get over.

While there are some things that irk me, like the typical no cap on the toothpaste that he squeezes from the top rather than the bottom, I realize that this sort of thing hardly matters. By simply buying two sets, the entire argument can be completely overlooked and forgotten. In terms of big things that confuse me or put me off, there are not really any.

The one thing that there is, it's not him. Luke

is very close to his family, and I've met them at their farmhouse in Kansas. I saw the way they make jokes back and forth to one another, the way that they bicker, but not in any sort of way that makes me think that there's any malice involved.

My own relationship with my family has been rather fraught. There were periods when my mom and I didn't talk much, and after his death, my father had become this big, looming presence in my life. Somebody who's watching over me, but not really. Somebody I think about.

When I talked to his fellow police officers, I started to believe that he had committed suicide. After this trip and everything being up in the air, I'm more confused than ever. My family comes with so much baggage. It's hard to know how to figure it all out.

The easygoing nature of his family has completely thrown me off. Could it really be that easy? Could you just get together and have a good time, support one another, be friends? I don't know. I don't really believe it fully, but maybe I have to start, because I'm going to be a part of it, after all.

Chapter 26

The thought of the drive to Big Bear Lake fills me with a mixture of dread and excitement. We land in LAX to a bright, sunny, warm winter day. It's in the mid-seventies and I quickly strip down to my t-shirt and revel in the feeling of the warm sun on my bare skin. I feel like I haven't seen the sun in weeks. Luke and I both smile ear to ear, popping into In-N-Out Burger and sitting outside while drinking our sodas and stuffing our mouths full of fresh-cut French fries.

We bask in the sunshine suddenly feeling like everything that happened back in the Pacific Northwest is nothing but a distant memory.

"It's funny how the weather has such an impact on my mood," I say. "Just sort of lifts my spirits and no matter how crappy things are, it feels like maybe it'll be okay, it'll work out in the end."

Luke smiles at me.

"In reality, everything worked out well, relatively. Think about what happened; I mean, the luck of finding Jodie and putting all the pieces together. We just have to wait to see what evidence they will find in the cabin. Things have really worked out. But I can't help but think about Cora and that case. The ex-husband is still a possibility."

"Chances are good this is the same Cora, but you can check in on it. Give Captain Carville a call."

We sit in comfortable silence for a few minutes.

"I'm going to miss you and the sunshine."

"Hey, the sun is going to shine in Big Bear Lake."

"Yeah, probably. I don't think there's any snow expected for another week or so, but I'm going to have to wear my coat again. I can't just be in a t-shirt like this."

"Well, you'll have more of a reason to come back then," he smiles, "because I'm going to miss you."

I keep these thoughts and the memories of being with him at the front of my mind as I make the almost three-hour drive back up to my hometown. A place that I both love and hate. The only place I had known until I was eighteen, and then the place that I always came back to with a heavy heart. This time I'm going to make some good memories. I'm going back to see my sister and to make things normal for her, as normal as they can possibly be. I have all the same questions that other people do.

How does she feel about her friend, Natalie, and the fact that she's gone? What about the man who took her? I'm not going to bring any of that up, not unless she does. This is going to be a time to start fresh. I drive up past the small communities of Running Springs and Green Valley Lake and make my way along the beautiful but winding road up to Boulder Bay, the beginning of Big Bear Lake.

There're some stunning five-thousand square foot houses perched right over the lake shore, surrounded by large, astounding boulders peeking out of the water.

I certainly remember the red house on the corner where I stop, waiting for the traffic to move at the light. This is one of the houses that my friends and I egged in high school on mischief night.

We were smart enough to leave our neighborhood and go further out, so that we wouldn't get caught. We decided to go with these bigger fancy houses because, well, we figured they could afford to have someone clean it up. We were brats, of course, not caring about the fact that we were destroying people's property and making them feel unsafe in their homes, but it was mischief night. It was almost Halloween. We had an excuse, right?

A bunch of other memories flood in. The little beach where my dad taught me how to swim. The park where my parents took me when I was a little girl and where I then took Violet when she was a toddler. The library that we passed just a few streets away, not visible from the main road, where Violet and I spent a lot of our time together. At some point through all of this, probably around the time when Mom and Dad started fighting nonstop and then after Dad's death, my mom had checked out. Somehow, she was able to be both overbearing and absent at the same time. When she was there, it was about her and what she wanted, and then she missed a bunch of other things when she was at home passing the time doing nothing.

I'm tempted to stop by a pub, an old favorite, to get myself some liquid courage, but I'm too excited to see Violet. Instead, I drive straight to my childhood home, a small two-bedroom cabin in Big Bear City nestled in close to all the other houses with small almost nonexistent backyards. For a little while, Violet and I shared a room, but I moved out when she was quite young and that room became hers.

My mom's old station wagon is parked out front. I pull my car to the curb halfway between Mrs. Thompson's house and ours, and Violet runs out toward me. I can't turn off the engine fast enough before taking her into my arms. We hold each other for a bit, and I let out a sigh of relief that she's actually put on a few pounds since the last time I saw her out there in the desert.

I don't let my mind go there. Finding her in that state was a horror beyond comprehension, something I never want to relive. When we pull away and look into each other's eyes, there's a knowingness there. I see her and she sees me and that we're sisters and we'll always be that way. Her hair has grown long; pulled up in a messy bun on top of her head. The dark color has grown out a little bit and her makeup is no longer thick charcoal around her eyes but it's enough to make her look like she's almost nineteen rather than fourteen.

I've always encouraged her to find her identity through how she looks, and she's experimented plenty. Mom, of course, wasn't too happy with some of the choices Violet made, but for someone who is into art as much as she is, I knew that was pretty inevitable. I just hoped that she would stop at hair color, makeup, removable things, and not dive headfirst into tattoos or any other body modification that would be permanent. Piercings I'm okay with; you can always take them out, so what's the big deal?

Violet is dressed in an oversized, long-sleeve t-shirt and the kind of baggy, boot-cut jeans that were popular in the late '90s. She looks like she got dressed from my old closet. In fact, I have to do a double take and try to think if these jeans with the ratty bottoms, full of slashes and tattered white strings that used to drive my mother nuts belonged to me or her.

"Is this a new pair of jeans?"

"Yes, I just got them. What do you think? Mom hates the fact that they're too long for my boots but, hey, that's the way you wear them, right?"

"That's the way I did." I smile, giving her a squeeze.

She has a couple of necklaces all intertwined. A locket, a stone attached to a thick black string that's strong around her neck, and a delicate star that sits in between her collarbones. A gift I got her when she turned twelve. Her hands are covered. When she grabs my hand and intertwines her fingers with mine, I touch the stacked rings and the ink pen illustration on her left hand.

"You drawing again?" I ask. "Making art?"

"Yes, of course," she says, "It's like asking if I'm breathing."

I smile. "That means you're doing well."

"Actually, I am. The therapist, I hate to say it and I probably will never tell Mom this, is really helping. Come on in. Mom's not here yet."

I smile. That explains her happy-go-lucky nature and how unbothered she seems.

"Have things gotten better with her and you recently?"

"Yes. To tell you the truth. Yes. She's been staying off my case about school for a bit. Got me the therapist, we've been watching TV together, just spending time together, and even did a puzzle."

"You did a puzzle? How uncool?"

"Oh, whatever."

"When you were a little girl, you used to love games," I say. "No matter how tired I was or no matter what anyone was doing, like you went through this phase where all you wanted to do was just play games, and it was fun."

"Oh, yeah, I bet I was a blast."

"No, you were. I mean, you were a lot to handle, but I liked you. I thought puzzles would appeal to you. Kind of difficult yet mindless; you could work on it for a little while and put it away."

"Yes. I haven't done one in ages, but Mom got one, at some yard sale if you can believe it. I was certain some pieces would be missing, but we started on it, and they're all there so far. Fingers crossed because it's got a thousand of them."

"A puzzle at a yard sale? That should be forbidden," I decide. "There's no way all the pieces are there. You want to make a bet on it?"

"Okay. Ten bucks."

"Let's make it five. I'm not so certain of my position."

Her bracelets dangle and make a loud jingling sound as we shake hands.

Inside, the house is as exactly as I remember. There's a fireplace in the corner, low ceilings, and an over-stuffed couch with a midcentury, modern side chair, and a wooden, carved coffee table, the kind that people buy for their vacation mountain houses. Mom had purchased it from the chainsaw artist who has a shop down the street. He focuses on bears, but he makes some rustic looking furniture as well.

The infamous thousand-piece puzzle is about halfway done depicting the lake and the ski slopes of Bear Mountain and Snow Summit. A powerboat racing creates white lines across the lake, and the snowcap mountains behind it with the ski slopes are clearly defined.

The one obvious thing wrong with it is that the ski slopes are on the side of the lake with the village, not the opposite side, the way that they're depicted in the puzzle, but that was probably done in an effort to convey everything about the town in one shot. Taking certain liberties is sometimes required.

"Come help me," she says.

Violet takes a seat on the shaggy carpet that's at least twenty years old. I leave my boots by the front door, take off my coat, hang it on the hook, and sit down on the opposite side of the table. I start looking for edge pieces. So far, this hasn't gone at all like I imagined, and it has been perfect. For a little while there, I worried that we'd have nothing to talk about.

That all I would think about was the last time I saw her: rescuing her from those horrible conditions, looking for her in vain for so long without much result. But being here, sitting and doing this puzzle changes everything. None of that stuff in the past matters. The only thing that matters is that she's alive, she's here, and she can be my sister again.

I ask her about school. She tells me how easy it is to do it online, no other kids to bother interacting with. No worries about anything.

"It's been fun being a recluse," she says. "I can see why you've done it for so long."

I want to roll my eyes and laugh, and then I don't hold back.

"That's what you were, right? You had like no

real friends, just did your own thing, boyfriend here and there."

"Yes, I guess I never thought of it that way," I say, feeling slightly embarrassed.

"Look, you have nothing to be worried about. That was just how you wanted to live life. You were obsessed with work and that's all you did. I want to do that. With school not taking up much time or thought now, I can really focus on my art. Even doing stuff like this is so relaxing, you know? I let my mind wander while I do something with my hands."

"Yes, I can see that," I say, "but it's important to have friends. I mean people to talk to and share with."

"Like the therapist."

"Yes. The therapist, of course, but people you don't pay to hang out with, and you don't even have to tell them about what happened or anything else. You just have a good time."

"Well, that's why I have you, my sister. Right? What are we going to do this weekend?"

"I was thinking the library, bowling alley, pizza place. Any other requests? Ice cream shop?" We both smile.

"We can't pass up Big Bear Scoops?"

"That place is my favorite," I admit.

"Those big milkshakes, they're delicious. How

about the ice cream sundae with cherries and chocolate syrup and strawberries?"

My mouth is watering. I smile. I find the missing piece from the top of the mountain with a little guy about to take off on a run and pop him into the puzzle.

"How about skiing? You want to go skiing, for old time's sake?"

"I don't know," she says after a pause. "Let me think about it."

Chapter 27

Jennifer Rivers liked to put up a harsh front with people she didn't know. She grew up that way. Her childhood was plagued by weekly moves to different hotel rooms and then various trailer parks. Whenever Mom and Dad couldn't make payments, they would pick up and leave. Move somewhere far away, start new. The one thing they never realized that Jennifer had learned when she was not even seven, was that no matter where you went, you brought yourself with you. Her parents, especially her mom, seemed to believe that a change of pace would somehow solve all her problems.

She would look forward to a new way of life. That things would be different in this new place. That *she* would be different. But then the alcohol would come. The stress of the move wouldn't dissipate. Her little Jenny was never quite quiet enough, never kept to herself enough. When she did, she was too quiet and too focused, which also drove her mom crazy. For the longest time, Jennifer, which is what she preferred to be called since she was sixteen years old, had lived life holding her breath. She tiptoed around her parents, then when it was just her mom, her and her boyfriends.

She tried for years to make herself invisible. That didn't work, because her mom would suddenly take an interest in her life out of the blue, and become involved, show up at school, make a scene, yell at her teachers. She never knew what to expect. The one time she came to the parent-teacher conferences and actually sat there, listened, and made nice, Jennifer had an anxiety attack back at home, stressed about what her mom would reveal to her teachers about her real home life.

When she got old enough, she debated calling social services, but she was always concerned that the place that she would go to would be worse. Then she'd have no control over anything. She knew enough about being poor and living on the cusp of total destitution, to know that there was no romance in running away. Staying here with a roof over her head was better than being out on the streets.

She had spent a few lonely nights out there when her mom had locked her out of her trailer. She sat on the stoop watching her neighbors and their drunken brawls, kicking one of the old men who tried to make passes at her before he eventually passed out from too many beers. That was plenty of street life.

She had watched the news and she knew what happened to young girls, and she was not going to be one of them. Instead, she stayed put, counting down the days to her eighteenth birthday, which was, luckily, when she was still in high school, because her mom had put her in school way too late. She'd considered trying to graduate early, but she liked school. It was eight hours of a safe place for her. She busied herself with as many clubs as possible: joining the newspaper staff, running track, laying out the yearbook, and even running for student council treasurer.

She wasn't one for making speeches. Instead, she liked running the numbers, staying quiet in the background. She always thought to herself that she probably should have been a librarian. She would've been happy there. Books were her happy place after all, but they required a master's degree in library sciences, and the pay hardly made up for the cost of the tuition.

She had decided that a government job with the FBI would be interesting enough and that it would be a good way to use her passion for criminology and behavioral psychology. Plus, it would set her up with a good retirement. Then maybe she could work at the library as a volunteer or something like that when she got older.

Jennifer approached all new work situations with her back up a little bit, being on guard, except for when she met Kaitlyn Carr. There were not too many women in this line of work, despite the considerable efforts made to hire and retain more. She wasn't officially on the job, but she liked how she got involved without stepping on anyone's toes.

There was something about her vibe, her energy. Jennifer hated the fact that she had even thought of that phrase. It felt too hippy for her. Like she was someone wearing a long dress talking about crystals and smoking too much marijuana. It was hard to find another way to describe it, though. As soon as they met, there was this chemistry, not romantic, but friendship. The beginning of one. Anyway, here was a kindred spirit, in the immortal words of *Anne of Green Gables*, one of her favorite childhood books. This person had understood her without her having to even explain a word. The rest of the people that she met were typical cops, small town without being hickish, honest, hardworking, but a little dense about the human condition, if you wanted to call it that.

They were supposed to figure out who had done it and put the pieces together, but it was Donald, the retired FBI agent, who seemed to have to pull them around on a short lead and to show them how it all worked. It was a difficult case that he had built, and there were lots of holes in it, she had to admit, and she wondered to herself whether she would've believed him if she had been in Kaitlyn's position. She had hoped that she would, but she had her doubts.

The main problem seemed to be that Donald was so eager that it bordered on zealotry. It made it difficult to take him seriously. He was like a person who had just found a new religion, proselytizing to anyone who would listen, about any angle that would bring them over to his side.

Now, when it came to Detective Clint Patterson, Jennifer wasn't so sure. He was an enigma. She liked his meticulousness and the fact that he was a little bit nerdy. Everybody else seemed like they were jocks or ex-jocks, but this guy actually talked about playing tabletop games and watching *Lord of the Rings*.

She liked how focused he was, and meticulous. He took notes on everything and seemed to make few judgments off the bat. This case would require that kind of reserve. He seemed to work well with others and didn't feel like her presence there as an FBI agent was a rebuke to his ability to do his job. There was no tussling for power because, well, she was frankly not interested in that anyway. She wanted to find a way for them to work together to put this guy in prison where he belonged.

Through her contacts, she was able to process the evidence from the cabin faster than the local labs would have managed. They found out that the prints found inside the cabin, besides the ones that belonged to Jodie, had belonged to someone who was not in the system.

They checked a number of databases, the typical ones where people are required to give their fingerprints. The ones people submitted to so they could get ahead of lines and airports like Clear and TSA Pre-Check, as well as statewide ones for any teaching instructional jobs, even volunteering at schools. Fingerprints were required for a lot of things nowadays. After going through as many databases as she could possibly think of and checking the nearby states, they found nothing. At least they had the prints. That was something.

The cabin itself was found to be registered to a woman named Celeste Griedier, and there was very little about her online except for her address, which was about ten miles away from David Trincia's home in Portland. Through tax records and social media, Jennifer was able to find out that

Celeste worked for Boyden, the same paper company in Portland that David did.

A huge find.

They had known each other, no doubt, and there was at least a connection to him being there, a tenuous one at that. At least there was someone to talk to now. Part of Jennifer was relieved that Kaitlyn and Luke were going back to Southern California. It would be improper to include them on the stakeout that she and Clint would be doing on David Trincia, trying to get his fingerprints. She wasn't sure whether they would expect an invitation. Thankfully, Donald also took the hint and returned back to Olympia, to his wife and his retirement, but only after a promise from her that he would be her first phone call about any news.

They were cooperating with the local precinct to make sure that everything that had been collected was processed and documented properly. Two vans were set up with surveillance equipment to take photos and video, but Jennifer and Clint were in a nondescript Honda Civic parked not too far away from David's home. She wasn't sure about his schedule or whether he had a tendency to go anywhere besides work and home. According to Donald and Kaitlyn, he didn't have a habit of going to any coffee shops, but of course they both hoped that he would make an exception.

After three long days in the car, boredom had overtaken anxiety, and Trincia had made no changes to his routine. Work, home, work, home. Went to two different clients in different parts of Portland, but ordered no food and stopped at no restaurants or shops on the way.

"This is going to be impossible." Jennifer turned to Clint when things were getting pretty dire.

"Not unheard of for these things to last weeks," he said, burying his head in his crossword puzzle.

It was her turn to be the lookout for the next two hours while he sat in the car and did his puzzles, and then they would trade off. She couldn't look away, not for longer than a few seconds, but she could listen to audio books. She had gone through six or so, running through all of her Audible credits long ago and being forced to buy more. Still, they waited and waited.

Chapter 28

Jennifer and Clint got along splendidly. It was not like they became friends, but acquaintances, partners. They got to know each other, learned little things about their lives outside of work without going into much depth. Clint wasn't exactly a sharer. He described some details about his life and the fact that he was fine being quiet and did not try to fill the time with jokes and other mindless chitchat was just fine by Jennifer.

She often found people exhausting, and though she was good putting up a front and being friendly and easygoing when the social situation required it, she nevertheless needed time to come home and decompress afterward, because it was nothing but an act. Other people, if they were to be asked, would find this surprising because she was so friendly and outgoing, but it was easier for her to be that way rather than be more standoffish and difficult and then deal with the repercussions.

Clint was good doing his puzzles for hours: Sudoku, crosswords, even Scrabble. They couldn't play together because then they would both be distracted, but they took turns. She was getting tired of the audio books and then took to her time off watching shows on Netflix, reading, and her newest hobby, embroidery. She wasn't someone who had a lot of hobbies, but she saw the embroidery ring for sale at the checkout of one of the online stores that she frequented. It was just an add on, completely unrelated to the rest of her purchase, but something told her to just buy it. It was only four bucks after all, and it came with everything she needed: the needles, the instructions, the thread.

She looked up a few stitches on YouTube since the instructions didn't exactly make much sense to someone who has never held a needle and thread in her hand. She liked it, the relaxing nature of it, the precision, and another two days later she was practically done with the elaborate but beginner design of a woman with flowers in place of her face. She even taught herself to do the daisy stitch, the lazy stitch, running stitch, blanket stitch, and the French twist, of which the lazy one was her favorite.

She only had half of one flower left and she

was having a little bit of a hard time because there was a mess of thread on the other side that she hadn't noticed until it was too late. She forced the needle through, pricking her thumb and saying ouch under her breath when Clint gasped and said, "There he is."

David Trincia was on his way from work. He had his briefcase, his poorly sized suit. His shoulders were slouched, and he looked tired, like he did most days when he left work. They had seen him on his client calls, however, and he definitely put up a front. Smiled, had a little bit of a swagger, broadened shoulders, and a completely different way of being in the world than he appeared now, just on his way to his car. Clint was good at following behind him, keeping a few cars in between them so as to not to draw attention.

Both Clint and Jennifer were expecting that he would just make his usual drive home, down Willow Boulevard over to Country Club and then down Morningside. But after almost a full seven days of watching him, he suddenly put on the blinker at Courant Avenue and Clint and Jennifer exchanged looks like, "This is new." They followed him closely and saw him pulling into the big box store plaza with Target at the head. He pulled in front of the T.J. Maxx, got out of his car, and went inside. Jennifer and Clint let out a sigh of disappointment. There was nothing that he could consume there and then toss away that they could use for prints. Thirty minutes later, he came out holding a bag of what looked to be clothes, got back into the car, and headed toward the exit.

"I really thought today was going to be the day," Jennifer said, not trying to hide her frustration. If he were leaving now, he would probably head home and that would be it. He would stay home the rest of the time and there was nothing they could do.

There was, of course, the option of going through his garbage, but there was a likelihood that the neighbors would spot them and they didn't want to draw any attention to themselves before they knew exactly what they were dealing with.

Out of nowhere, just before he exited the plaza, he pulled up to the drive-through window of the French Café, a fancy coffee stand that had just been built less than a few months ago. Clint parked in the Petco parking lot across the lot and watched as he went around, got his order, and then turned and headed to Target.

They didn't follow him into the store, but parked ten cars down and held their breath while he shopped. They had watched him walk inside holding a coffee cup in his hand, and the one thing that was on their mind was whether or not he would throw it out inside the store.

There were garbage bins everywhere. This was a strong possibility.

They sat on pins and needles, waiting. Jennifer fiddled with the radio until finally Clint asked her to turn it off.

The silence was deafening. Their eyes bounced back and forth from his car to the entrance as if looking more intently would make him suddenly appear out of thin air.

About half an hour later, he did, plastic coffee cup in hand. He was laden down with two heavy bags and the way that he held the cup, Jennifer knew that it was almost empty. He had fiddled with it a little bit the way you do to check how much of the coffee was still left, then grabbed the rim and tossed it into the garbage can.

They watched him walk all the way back to his car, waiting a few moments for him to leave before Jennifer turned to Clint and said, "I guess I'll go get it."

They had waited so long that it was almost like it was a surprise that it had happened at all. David Trincia was long gone, but his purple and yellow French Country Cafe to-go coffee cup with the unmistakable yellow fleur-de-lis on one side was difficult to miss.

Jennifer pulled on her gloves and placed the cup carefully into a box, not a plastic bag, the way that is typically done in television dramas. It had rained outside. The humidity was horrendous and fingerprints and other biological evidence are susceptible to humidity and degradation. Plastic bags are not ideal for things like that, especially if you place the evidence in directly. The box was a perfect fit and provided a secure barrier for the coffee cup itself and whatever DNA evidence it had, protecting it from the evidence bag that she then placed the entire contents into and sealed.

She signed it, Clint signed it. The date was placed. When this would be unsealed later in the lab, the tech would carefully sign off as well, and mark the time and date to preserve the chain of evidence for court.

For now, Jennifer held it in her lap and she and Clint smiled ear to ear, saying nothing, but silently giving thanks for the fact that in this situation, whatever gods existed or did not, they were working in their favor.

Chapter 29

By the time that Mom came home that evening, Violet and I were in such a good mood that not even she could have spoiled it. Smiling broadly, Mom came in carrying takeout and gave me a warm hug even though I had given her very little notice that I was coming. She was genuinely happy to see me and didn't put on a guilt trip about how little I visited her.

Instead, the three of us have an utterly, remarkably unremarkable evening playing board games and finishing the lake puzzle. Surprisingly, there were enough pieces and now I owed Violet five dollars. We have Thai takeout, gorge ourselves on way too many helpings, and then lie around the couch watching an old favorite, *Hocus Pocus*, even though it is well after Halloween.

It happened to be on cable, but we had

already missed half of it. Mom offers to put it on streaming and we start from the beginning. With my bladder bursting, I tell them to pause it right before Bette Midler begins to sing. I run to the bathroom, only then reflecting on what a wonderful evening this has been: simply pleasant, fun, without any undue pressures, anxiety, or expectations.

When I return, Mom and Violet are laughing, fighting over the popcorn, and Violet shows her how she strings it to make sure that the kernels don't fall apart. Again, it's like we're making up for lost holidays because it's way past Christmas. I grab a handful, spill a few on my shirt, and plop down next to them on the couch, touching my mom slightly.

She leans over, gives me a smile, and I'm overcome by the feeling of wanting to give her a hug and a big thank you for not ruining it, but I know that merely saying that would ruin the moment. Instead, I smile and settle for the quick embrace. She kisses the top of my head like she did when I was a kid, and I start to think to myself that perhaps this relationship is salvageable. Perhaps now that Violet is back, anything is possible.

Maybe we can be a different family. Everything can be different because she has come back, and that means we can start life again. The pessimistic part of me starts to say that people don't change, but I quickly shut it down. Things are different. Today is different. Maybe if we expect a little less and are grateful for a little bit more, we can have decent relationships with people who we don't wholly understand and probably never will. When the movie comes to a close, Violet is asleep on my mom's shoulder and Mom doesn't get up to move, not one inch.

Instead, she points to the blanket that had fallen to her ankles and asks me to wrap it around both of them. I tuck them in, and Mom remains sitting, enjoying her moment with her teenage daughter, a moment that she probably hasn't had in a long time. I grab another handful of popcorn, the kernels that haven't popped all the way, the leftovers, tossing them in my mouth just as my phone begins to vibrate.

"I have to take this," I whisper, excusing myself to Violet's room so that I can talk at full volume.

"It's a match," Jennifer Rivers says, not able to contain the excitement in her voice. "His fingerprints are a match to the ones found inside the cabin. We're going to arrest him now."

"Right now?" I ask.

"Yes. We have patrol officers sitting outside his house. We were waiting for these preliminary results to get the warrant."

"We're picking up Celeste Griedier as well,"

Jennifer beams. "Going to get her statement, especially now that we have the fingerprints. It changes everything. This case is breaking as we speak, Kaitlyn, and you are part of that."

"Oh, I'm so relieved," I say. "Part of me wishes I was up there."

"No, you don't. It's going to be a lot of paperwork, a lot of talking, and it's going to take a while for anything to develop anyway, as you know."

"Well, I wish I could be there when you pick him up and read him his rights."

"Yes, that's going to be pretty sweet," Jennifer says, and I can sense her smiling through the phone. "Okay, I've got to go, just wanted to touch base. I'll keep you updated about any developments."

"Thanks. I appreciate it." I hang up. I stare at my phone for a few moments as it goes blank. I tell myself, "This is finally over. We caught him."

Chapter 30

As soon as the warrant was in hand, Clint and Jennifer set out for David's house. Clint put on the lights and drove as fast as he could. The patrol car was there watching, making sure Trincia didn't go anywhere. Neither of them had a bad feeling about it, things were finally going to be coming due. Another detective was in the process of picking up Celeste Griedier. She hadn't been notified about anything, and she would be kept in the dark in order to keep her talking for as long as possible.

Jennifer nervously cracked her fingers on the drive over and then, becoming aware of how she was acting by the glance that Clint had given her, she stopped, suddenly self-conscious. Over the course of almost a week together in the car, she had gotten to know her temporary partner quite well, and yet not at all. It wasn't that he was a mystery, it was that he didn't feel like sharing much. That was okay with her until this moment when she felt like they needed to celebrate, to somehow acknowledge what was about to happen.

Clint gave off the same serious, inscrutable expression that he had given off the entire stake-out. What she did know about him was that they didn't like any of the same music. Listening to something at this moment was out of the question, but the silence in the car was uncomfortable for Jennifer, who usually listened to audiobooks or her favorite playlist on loop. She would even settle for a podcast, anything to keep her mind somewhere else. Clint, on the other hand, seemed to be enjoying the silence.

It was a dark night and the streetlights illuminated their path. As they turned onto his street, they anticipated seeing a patrol car parked in front of his house. However, when they arrived, there was no sign of law enforcement, not even a vehicle parked to the side.

"Where the hell is he?" Clint asked.

They were supposed to have someone here. He pulled up and stepped briskly on the brakes, pushing her forward into her seat belt.

They jumped out of the car and ran toward the front door. They knocked once and grabbed the knob. It was open. They ran inside, but it was empty. No one was home.

━━━

D avid Trincia was nowhere to be found. Jennifer and Clint ran into his modest craftsman house, guns drawn, ready for anything, including their suspect fleeing the arrest, but what they were not ready for was his disappearance. They checked every bedroom, rushed to the backyard, made frantic calls to their superiors for backup, secured the perimeter, all to no avail.

David Trincia was missing. What they had not known was that David Trincia had been tipped off that the cops were watching him. He was a careful man who never threw away his to-go cups in public garbage cans, except on the one occasion when he stopped by Target on a whim to buy some toothpaste and a few other personal items.

Stopping by the French Country Cafe, the drive-through window, was another one of those last-minute decisions that he would grow to regret, especially after the call came that somebody was looking into him. He saw the patrol car sitting at the edge of the street from the inside of his home. He had no idea what the cops knew and what they didn't, and he had no knowledge that the FBI was involved as well. He had seen a few similar cars sitting outside his office and thinking back, he realized that they were probably conducting surveillance, but he was too cocky to admit that earlier on.

David Trincia had been getting away with murder for more than fifty-five years. There were not just the cases that Donald C. Clark had pieced together. There were others as well. The ones that he never mentioned to his nephew. The only one that still haunts him was the first; when he was fifteen and he killed his best friend.

He had asked him to go to the woods after school on a regular Wednesday afternoon. In fact, they had been there before; smoked some pot, talked about girls, and looked at stolen Playboy magazines from the local gas station. On that particular afternoon, David had gotten hold of a six-pack of beers and the two of them got drunk together talking about their crushes at school.

Benjamin Garp, Benny, as everyone had called him, was friendly, popular, and outgoing. Some of his jock friends from the track team had asked him why he still hung out with David Trincia, the quiet kid with a slouch, bad acne, and a seeming inability to put even a few sentences together when called on in class, but Benny was a loyal friend. They had been close friends since kindergarten. Back when their moms were friends and took them to the playground together. When he reached his teenage years, David got a little weird, but that was something that Benny had hoped to help his friend with.

It was afternoons like this when Benny thought 'this is the reason I'm friends with him.' But it was not the procurement of alcohol or drugs that made this version of David attractive. It was that when he was a little bit buzzed, he seemed to forget how shy he was and came out of his shell. He would make raunchy jokes and laugh just as hard as any of the cool guys on Benny's track team. It was this guy that he had hoped that his other friends would be able to see some time.

Unbeknownst to David, Benny was planning a party at his house when his parents were going to be away for the weekend. It had grown so big that practically the whole school was invited. Benny had purposely kept the information from David in hopes that he would spring it on him on Friday at lunch. That way, David wouldn't have too much time to worry about all the things that could go wrong and show up.

Benny knew his friend well. He thought he knew what was best for him, but his friend had a secret. Many secrets in fact. David wasn't as shy and cowardly as he had wanted his friend to believe. He had already kissed a girl and more when he drove his car to the wrong side of town and picked up a prostitute at the truck stop. She had shown him what to do, and everything that he had been missing in his life. To share all this information with Benny, his closest friend, was unthinkable.

The party that Benny didn't think he knew about, he had been hearing about since Monday. The school was abuzz with it, excited because there would be a keg. Everyone talked freely around David because he was an overweight nerd with few friends and was easy to ignore when he buried his face in thick science fiction novels at lunchtime and in class.

What would happen that fateful Wednesday would come as a little bit of a surprise to David even though he had planned out most of it. This was another thing that he had never done before but had been thinking about since he was about nine.

What would it be like to kill a person?

What would it be like to extinguish life from their body and watch death come over them?

He had seen plenty in movies, read about it in books but there was nothing like the real thing.

David had brought a few different weapons with him to the woods behind the school; a knife, a tie to use if he wanted to strangle him, and an icepick. He had no access to a gun, which was probably for the best because he wasn't sure that he could get a gun that was untraceable.

After smoking a joint and drinking too many beers, both boys started acting inebriated and slow. Neither of them was particularly experienced in that arena, but Benny was far more affected by all the substances than David, who had secretly poured out one and a half of the beers when Benny wasn't looking. It was at that point that Benny tried to get up and walk around, unable to put one foot in front of the other he fell down laughing. That was when David saw his opportunity.

He jumped on his friend, straddling him and pinning him down. At first, Benny thought that it was just a wrestling move. He tried to toss him off, but he couldn't. Another thought that popped in his head was that maybe David was making a move on him. There were rumors at school that David was gay, which Benny had never believed until this moment.

"Get off of me," he said, slurring his words. But David didn't. Instead, he grabbed Benny's head, pulling it forward and off the ground, then let it drop.

Benny felt his brain rattle around inside his skull. He tried to push David off, and even managed to punch him in the face, bloodying his nose. David pulled on two sides of the silk tie that Benny had bought at Goodwill the day before and cut off oxygen to Benny's airways.

At first, Benny thought that his friend was just joking, a sick joke, trying to scare him maybe, but that was it. He wasn't actually trying to strangle him, was he? He had no idea.

He struggled, scratched David's arms, tried to reach for his neck, but he was growing weaker with every moment. As far as strangulation itself goes, David was surprised how long it took. In movies, it was over in a few seconds and with every passing minute, his arms were growing weaker and weaker but he held on tight. Eventually, Benny lost consciousness and stopped fighting, but David didn't.

He had held the ties even tighter for a good ten minutes just to make sure that Benny couldn't come back. Then his best friend in the whole world was gone. Afterward, David checked for his footprints and covered them up. Luckily, it hadn't rained for two days and there was no mud in the woods. He took the tie with him. He took the empty beer cans and the leftover piece of the joint. He took all the evidence that he could think of and left Benny where he was.

He was found by the track team, by Benny's true friends, early the following morning on their before-school run. The sight of his dead body would stay with each one of those seven boys for the rest of their lives. Some would even see him again on their deathbeds.

As far as the investigation went, no one knew a thing. The local police hadn't dealt with a murder in more than five years, and before that, it was just a few domestic abuse cases, which were easy to figure out because it was always the husband. They did come and talk to David twice, and he did say that they had a habit of going into the woods, but he hadn't gone there this week. He was properly distraught, perfectly fitting the part of someone who had lost their best friend.

The local police just couldn't believe that anyone in their small community, let alone Benny's best friend, no matter how odd he had seemed to the outsiders, could be responsible for anything like this. It was an impossibility, completely unthinkable. Besides, there was no evidence pointing in his direction whatsoever.

A few girls were even interviewed because people had heard that he had gone there with one or two high school friends. After much coaxing, the girls had finally admitted that they were there two months ago, that they had let him go to second base, but nothing else happened. When they said no, he didn't pressure them anymore.

For a few months there, David had worried a little bit that he might be caught, but then he realized how set in their illusions everyone was about him, and if he just pretended to live a life of virtue, no one would think twice because no one would ever suspect a thing.

As for the evidence, he had burned all of it; all except for a little piece of the tie that he had used. He couldn't bring himself to burn that. He had to keep some kind of memento. Of course, he had to be safe with it. Perhaps there were fingerprints. They could be taken off of it, and if not now, maybe in the future. The things he read in the science fiction books told him that anything was possible in the future, and he would have to be prepared for it, especially if he wanted to do it again. And again. And again.

Chapter 31

After it was discovered that David Trincia was gone and that he had the time to pack a few items into a suitcase to take with him, the hammer came down hard on the patrol officers who were supposed to be watching his home. Luckily, they had a good reason to leave.

There was a shooting just a few blocks away and they were the closest car to the location. A child had picked up a gun and shot his father in the leg, and thanks to the patrol officer's quick thinking by putting pressure on the wound, the paramedics were able to save him from bleeding out. Jennifer Rivers and Clint Patterson were pissed off, angry, but there was only so much they could say after they found out what had happened.

The question now was, where was David Trincia?

An APB, an all-points bulletin, was put out on his vehicle and law enforcement agencies in both states were on the lookout for a dangerous, likely armed criminal, who was supposed to be taken into custody right away.

Of course, there were regrets. Jennifer was upset with herself more than anyone for not staking out his house and staying there until the prints came back, but it had been a long week and there were no guarantees. Clint didn't say much because he never said much, but he felt bad as well.

He knew that they had made a mistake, one they wondered if they could ever fix. In the meantime, they did have Celeste Griedier, his coworker from Boyden, and the person who was listed as the owner of the cabin to take their anger out on. But if they were to go in hot like they were now, nothing good would happen.

A new plan was made. Clint was going to be the main investigator asking all the questions. Jennifer was going to stay back and watch from the camera and come in only if extra pressure was needed, the kind of pressure that was brought on by the introduction of an FBI agent.

Celeste was a mousey woman with dark brown

hair, minimal makeup, and scared, beady eyes that darted around the room. She cowered in her seat, barely moving, hunched over and cradling the coffee cup that she had accepted from Detective Clint Patterson because, well, frankly, she couldn't say no.

Despite the worries in the back of his mind that he wouldn't be able to contain his frustration, he started out politely. He asked her about her relationship with David Trincia, and she said that they were colleagues. Sometimes they would have lunch together, but she worked in accounting, and he was in sales.

"How is he as an employee?"

"Good, he's one of the top performers," she said. "Gets a lot of bonuses. He used to travel all the time, but he's been wanting to take some time off."

"Does he have a family?"

"No, it's just him. He and his wife got divorced. They never had any children."

"How long were they together?" Clint asked.

"Five, no, seven years. They dated for a bit, had a small wedding at the Justice of the Peace. None of us really knew her well, but she came to some of the holiday parties, picnics, that kind of thing. David was a friend."

"What is David like?"

"Friendly, outgoing. Sometimes he tries too hard to make friends, but I got to know him a little better and I could see that that was a facade. He was really shy in real life."

"Any hobbies or is it just work?"

"He likes to watch true crime documentaries, read science fiction, loves all those Marvel movies, *Star Wars*, nothing out of the ordinary."

"What about you?"

"No, that's not my thing."

"So how come you guys got so close?"

"I didn't say that." Celeste almost shuddered at the thought. "He just kept coming around. Neither of us liked this one other salesperson and we made jokes about him for a bit, so we connected over that, and then we had lunch together. I like true crime, too, so we'd talk about different documentaries on Netflix and all those shows, like *20/20,* or *Forensic Files.* There's not a lot of men who are into that stuff, so it's nice. My husband hates it."

"It was never romantic between you two?"

"No, not at all. I'm married, I have children," she clarified.

"He is in his late sixties, right?"

"Actually, he's seventy-one," she said.

"Still working?"

"Yes, we have a lot of clients who like having

older people show up and talk to them. They've been around for many years, so he handles a lot of those cases. He was thinking of retiring off and on at different times. Getting out of the cold rain, maybe moving to Arizona or Florida. He could do it, too. I mean, he doesn't spend much and he lives pretty modestly in that house that he's had forever. It's all paid off already."

"He told you that?" Clint asked.

She nodded. "His whole thing was, what would he do without work? He already watches a lot of TV, has a lot of time to read, so he just didn't want to give up his job. He kept putting it off, and he stays pretty fit. Hasn't had any heart problems, nothing like that."

Clint took careful notes in his notepad even though the whole interview was getting recorded, but it's not the substance that he was writing down. It was his impressions, her demeanor, the way she answered the questions, so that he had something to refer to when watching the tape, and to see if anything's different.

"Okay, so tell me about the cabin," Clint said.

Her eyes opened wide. She stared at him, partly uncertain as to how to respond.

"What cabin?" She pretended that she didn't know what he was talking about, but it was too late. Clint gave her a smirk.

"You know what cabin, the one registered in your name."

Her mouth went dry, parched. She licked her lips, but it didn't help. She took a few sips of her coffee and that did nothing either. She knew that the cabin would come back to haunt her at some point and that was why she didn't want to do it.

Now it was here, and she didn't know the best way to reply. Should she have told him the truth? Then what if David found out, should she have lied? She wondered, but then she realized that she had no idea the extent to which the police were aware of the place. They clearly knew that she was the owner, but what else did they know?

"It's better if you tell us the truth. We know a lot, a lot about the cabin," Clint said, trying to be patient. "It's in your best interest to cooperate with us because, as you may or may not know, David is a very bad guy."

Her heart sank. She stared at the indentations in the Formica table in front of her. This, she did not know. David Trincia was her friend. A little bit shady, a little bit squirrely, secretive even, but she never suspected that he was bad. No, not in any way. Celeste shifted her weight from one side to another. She didn't know how to get herself out of this. She wanted to be anywhere but here, but that was not an option. Should she ask for a lawyer? Would that make things worse?

"Tell me about the cabin, Celeste," Clint said, reaching over the table, touching her arm, and making her jump in her seat. "Tell me everything you know."

———

Celeste hesitated some more, but Clint wasn't letting it go. He asked her about the cabin again, and on the third time she gave in.

"David asked me to put the cabin in my name," she said. "It was the truth."

Perhaps she should have gotten a lawyer, but she just wanted the questioning to stop, not be prolonged even further.

"Isn't that unusual?" Clint asked.

"Yes, I thought it was, but he talked to me about it a number of times. He said he didn't want his family to know. He said that he had family that he wasn't close to, and he did not want this cabin to go to them in the event of his death. He brought it up a number of times. He said that I would owe him nothing. It would just be in my name."

"Why couldn't he rent it?"

"He wanted to own it. He paid for it upfront, I believe. Cash. Maybe a hundred thousand dollars. I don't know. I never checked. I didn't want to worry about it. I finally agreed. I never told my husband. He wouldn't have wanted me to do it. He would've suspected that there was something going on between me and David, but there wasn't. I wanted nothing to do with this cabin. He just wanted to put it in my name because he was worried that if something happened to him, his family would get it."

"Why didn't he just write a will excluding them from the property?"

"I suggested that, but he didn't want to cause more trouble. That's what he said. He just didn't want them to know. He put my name on the deed, and every year he paid all the property taxes and all the upkeep. I'm assuming he used it sometimes. Though, he never talked about it, not in the office. Whenever I would bring it up, he would remind me that he didn't want anyone to know, and so we kept it that way."

Clint looked at Celeste, eyeing her, analyzing her body language, wondering if he believed a word of what she was saying. There would only be one question that would confirm his suspicions. He took his time phrasing it, took a sip of his coffee, and looked her up and down. She trembled at his gaze and looked away.

"We found a woman who he had kept in the cellar underneath that cabin for months; starved her, raped her, abused her. Would you know anything about that?"

Celeste's eyes shot up. They got big. They turned into large silver dollars and her pupils dilated. She sat up straight. The horror on her face was unmistakable.

"What are you talking about?" She managed to utter. "No, no, what?"

Chapter 32

Unlike Clint Patterson, Jennifer Rivers wasn't so
sure that Celeste Griedier was telling the truth.
Yes, she was shocked and astonished by what Clint
had revealed to her, but she wasn't face-to-face
and the camera from the top angle only conveyed
Celeste's reaction partly. When Clint gave Celeste
a breather and left her alone to see what she
would do and to talk to the people upstairs in the
audio-visual room, he came in practically with his
mouth open.

"She's telling the truth," he said. "I know it."

Jennifer tried to protest, but he was adamant.

"You should have seen her reaction," Clint
said.

"Their reactions are always Oscar-worthy. You
know why?" Jennifer asked. "Because their lives
are on the line. If she knew about that girl, she's

an accessory and accomplice, maybe worse, a willing participant. Now she can just have deniability."

"I get the sense that she was telling the truth," Clint added.

It was an understatement and a measured one, but Jennifer knew Clint well enough to know that exaggeration was not his forte.

The fact that he had believed Celeste so wholeheartedly had made her question her own thoughts and opinions that she had just moments ago held so dearly. Could she be mistaken?

Perhaps he was right. She wasn't there. That was where she wanted to be. Watching on the video camera was not the same thing as looking a suspect in the eyes. It was not the same thing as seeing the little beads of sweat and perspiration on their forehead, the way they fidgeted even when they tried not to. All that stuff was partly lost to the camera because its position was static, coming from one direction.

It didn't allow you to really be a part of the room. Clint went through his impressions, and Jennifer and the rest of the people in the room listened carefully.

"Do we believe the fact that her husband doesn't know about the cabin?" Jennifer asked.

"I want to say yes." Clint nodded. "She looked terrified. She was the one who had asked David not to tell him, and this would be an easy thing to figure out. So far, I think she's telling the truth. Maybe she's a little naïve, maybe she believed her friend, maybe she got tired of him pestering her about it. She did say that she brought it up to him at work and he shot her down because he didn't want anyone else to know, so it was a little secret, one that she probably put out of her mind."

"Had she ever been there?" Jennifer asked.

"No, I didn't ask yet, but I will."

"I want to come with you," Jennifer said.

Clint hesitated.

"She started to cave when you became more forceful. She's not someone who makes friends," Jennifer insisted. "She'll respond positively when she learns who I am."

Clint was still uncertain of that fact, but he knew how desperately Jennifer wanted to participate. He was certain of the regrets that she felt about what had happened to David Trincia and the fact they'd both let him get away. Anyway, it wouldn't be a bad idea to have someone else on his side saying that Celeste Griedier should be believed.

They decided to bring some offerings of goodwill, a few snacks from the vending machine to put her at ease: a pack of pretzels, a bag of M&M's, and Skittles. They weren't sure which one she would prefer. Jennifer decided that she was going to have whichever one was left because her stomach was still rumbling and there was not going to be any time for lunch.

Armed with sugar, stern faces, and fresh cups of coffee, Jennifer and Clint went back into the interrogation room. What Clint had realized was that Jennifer was right. As soon as she had said, "Special Agent FBI," Celeste started to shake visibly and perspire. Her hands even left little sweat stains on the table. She tried to wipe them off so that no one would see, but they had both noticed.

As for the snack, she reached for Skittles, a surprise to both Clint and Jennifer, and eagerly bit into the bag, tossing a few colorful candies in her mouth. The explosion of sugar gave her a little peace and calm, but it was only temporary because when she looked back up, she saw Jennifer and Clint staring at her.

"You have to believe me. I knew nothing about the cabin, I've never been there," Celeste said. "My name was just on the deed, but I wanted nothing to do with it. That way if my husband ever found out, I could say there was nothing to know because I didn't know anything. At first, I thought he would find out and he would think that I was having an affair, but time passed and I kind of forgot. David never wanted to talk about it, and so we didn't."

Jennifer was still not entirely convinced, but she promised herself that she would keep an open mind. They were there to hear the truth in whatever form it would be, and if she refused to say it, they'd stay as long as it would require.

Chapter 33

The day is as perfect as it can be. A little bit of frost is in the air, the skies are blue, and a few puffs of clouds are high up, voluminous, without any threat of rain or snow. The two Carr girls have done all their favorite things, the pizza parlor, the library, the movie theater, and even the bowling barn. The day is one for the books; one neither of us will soon forget. We laugh and then we laugh some more. Make sarcastic remarks about tourists walking up and down the village. Even though we have not been apart that long, we both revel in our time together.

I can't believe how Violet has changed from the bruised lost girl that I found in the desert to the almost happy-go-lucky teenager who is enjoying her days probably even more than she had before. I suspect that she is putting on an act, of course, being the best version of herself in front of me. Then later, at home, she will return to her cocoon away from people and try to recuperate, but I hope that perhaps a big part of this is real.

The longer that the day goes on, the more I realize that in fact, it is. My sister is enjoying spending time with me. She is happy to see me, and that means everything. That is the whole reason I am here. Despite the day, or perhaps because of it, I never bring up what happened to her. It stays on the back burner in a secret compartment. It will only be let out if Violet brings it up first. At least that is my decision early on. Later I start to doubt myself. Perhaps I should have brought it up, given her an opportunity to talk about it, not put all the onus on her.

The day goes on. The fun is had, and I just don't want to ruin it. I want to be here in the moment, enjoy it for what it is, make memories out of fleeting moments that I had thought would be impossible to make again.

Right after we finish dinner at our favorite Himalayan restaurant and while we are waiting for dessert, Jennifer calls me over FaceTime. Reception isn't too great inside the place, so I excuse myself and head outside to talk on the curb.

"Thanks for FaceTiming," I say. "It's good to see you in person."

"Yes, I figured."

"It's been a bit."

"We have a lot to catch up on," Jennifer says.

She's at home. Her hair is pulled up in a bun. She looks a little bit tired but smiling, nevertheless.

"We've been talking to Celeste Griedier, as you know."

"How's that going?"

She had texted me a little bit about it, but I'm glad that we could have an actual conversation.

"At first, I didn't believe it when Clint talked to her, but then I was in the room, and she seems to have no knowledge about Jodie Schmidt being at the cabin. She had never been there before. Her name was just on the deed, and she seemed to know nothing."

"She didn't think it was weird that he would want to put a cabin in her name?" I ask.

"Yes, she did, but he insisted; he kept pestering her about it. She was terrified about her husband finding out. She didn't want him to think that she was having an affair or anything like that."

"You really think she's telling the truth?"

"We found no fingerprints of hers anywhere in that place. The ones we found were confirmed to be his or Jodie's. We're checking the cameras to see if we could spot her car in the vicinity, but she seemed to have put it in her name a while ago and just put it out of her mind. It was hard for me to believe as well, but when I talked to her face-to-face, I could tell that Clint was right. She is, in all likelihood, telling the truth and until we find some evidence otherwise, I think we have to believe her."

"Okay," I say. Not exactly going along with the proposition, but feeling like I don't really have many other options. "What about Trincia? Where is he?"

"We still have no idea."

"None?"

"The car seems to have disappeared. Someone tipped him that we were coming and he took off in it, but he likely switched cars soon after. He had a plan. He is a smart guy."

"Yes, but even smart guys make mistakes," I say.

"That's what we're hoping for. Everyone that we know he knows through work, clients, the gym that he goes to, everywhere else have been notified to keep an eye out. Everyone thinks he's a great guy, but they promised to call if he showed up. So far he hasn't been in touch with anyone."

"Does he have any other passports, driver's licenses?"

"Not that we found at the house, but maybe he doesn't keep them at the house. His name's plastered all over the agency's bulletin boards. We've notified law enforcement departments up and down the West Coast. I'm getting to work and getting him onto the FBI's most wanted list, but it takes time, approvals, that type of thing, as you can imagine. Otherwise, every guy out there would be on it."

"What's your feeling about it?" I ask. The light from the headlights wraps around me with each passing car. I'm shivering and my teeth are chattering because I forgot my coat, but I'll talk to her for however long it takes.

"I think we're going to find him. Obviously, the more time that passes the more likely it is that he gets out of the state, out of the country. We have people down in Mexico, all the resorts, the usual places. Now, if he stays low, uses cash, I don't know. He'll be a hard one to find. People make mistakes and we'll be there."

"I just hope that we can find him before there's another murder."

"That's my hope as well, but--"

"Sorry. I didn't mean it like you're not doing a good job. I know you're doing your best."

"I have a lot of regrets about how we handled it. Those patrol cops, they shouldn't have been there. They did everything right. They saved someone's life. I was the one who should have stayed behind. Sometimes you have to do the job yourself in order to get it done."

"There was a shooting. You can't blame yourself for that."

"You don't know me." She gives me a wink. "I can blame myself for all sorts of things that I have no personal responsibility for. It's a gift."

I chuckle. We promise to stay in touch and keep each other updated.

I hang up, rub my hands together, and stare at the warm yellow light emanating from inside the restaurant. Violet didn't bother waiting for me to start on the Gulab Jamun, a deep-fried dough ball drizzled with honey. I'm just about to grab the door when my phone vibrates in my hand and I answer it before really glancing down at the screen. "Jennifer?" I ask.

"Hey, it's me. Anthony Leonelle."

My mouth drops open. It's too late to hang up to ignore the call. Yet I don't have the energy or the willingness to talk to him right now.

"Can you talk?" he asks in a sweet, thin voice and I can't resist.

"Yes. What's going on?"

"My dad did it. I know it," he says. "That's why he wants her cremated."

"Is she going to be?"

"No, no thanks to him. I'm using the money

she saved for my college for her burial. But he's not happy about it."

I let out a sigh of relief. This was a big spot of contention and I'm glad that Theodor Rydell caved and let him bury his mother.

"I know that he was involved."

"I'm not so sure, Anthony. We have gone over this a few times and so have the cops investigating his case."

Everyone had agreed that with an alibi that was now gone, his father was likely the one who was responsible for the murder of his mother. The cops are now trying to make a case. That's why he hasn't been arrested yet. They're working on it.

"There's a lot that they know that they can't reveal yet. They're going to get to the bottom of it."

"No, they're not. They're just going to let them go."

"Listen, I don't think your father did it," I say. "There's another man who might have been responsible."

"Who?"

"He's a serial killer. There are three different murders that were tied to him, and the authorities are currently working on putting all the pieces together. It's either your father and, because his wife is now no longer saying that he was with her, there is the possibility that it was him, but it could be this other guy that we've been investigating all along. I don't know for sure."

"I don't care about this other guy. I don't care what my stepmother is now saying. My dad was stalking my mom and he killed her. He didn't want her to be with Steve. He didn't want her to move away with me. He wanted her under his thumb. That's why he was saying that she was an escort, spreading all of those lies about her."

"Your father was in another relationship. I wouldn't call--"

"Yes, he's married, but he's a cheater," Anthony says.

I haven't talked to him for a while, but I'm drawn to him right away the way I was when I first met him, and he pled for me to help him figure out what happened. I was the one who had found his mother, Cora Leonelle, murdered and hung in that tree. I was the one who had made him promises; ones I couldn't keep, and I definitely shouldn't have made.

"I'm not talking about your stepmother," I say.

"My father was having an affair with my mother?"

"No, another woman, he was lying to your stepmother, and he was probably with this other woman that night. I can call Captain Carville again and let you know what they can tell you. They can't reveal that much because they're trying to build a case and it always looks like they're not doing anything until it comes out in court. That's just the way it has to be handled. Otherwise, important evidence is going to slip out and it can taint their investigations and interviews with other witnesses."

"You see, he is an ass. He was cheating on Melinda. He cheated on my mom. He just wanted to control all these women. You know that he wasn't letting my stepmom out to do shopping. He was watching her every move and all throughout that he was still cheating. Do you know what it's like to live with a guy like that? He's been trying to control me my whole life, and he was trying to control my mom, too. I don't care. You think this other guy did it? Some nameless serial killer. I don't care. I know that my dad did it and I'm finally going to do something about it."

"What are you talking about, Anthony?" I ask. A chill that has nothing to do with the wind makes me shudder.

"I'm going to do something about it just like I should have done instead of waiting for you people to get it together. I'm going to take him out."

"Anthony, what does that mean?"

"I'm going to make him pay for what he did."

"Anthony, don't do anything stupid."

"I'm not going to. I'm going to get away with it just like he has."

"No, you won't. Are you talking about killing him?" I ask. No response. "You want to kill your father and now you're telling me that you're going to do it. You're not going to get away with it. You might kill an innocent man."

"He's not innocent."

"Yes, he's an asshole. He's a liar. He's a terrible, terrible person who is controlling and treats you like crap, but that doesn't make him a killer. In fact, there's a strong possibility that he had nothing to do with her death. Taking the law into your own hands is just going to get you twenty, thirty years in prison for something that never should have happened."

"Well, you better take care of it."

"What do you want me to do, Anthony?" I ask again after a long pause.

"There's nothing you can do. I'm going to hang up now."

"No, don't, Anthony, don't. Please don't kill your father. Please don't even try. Please think about this. You have your whole future ahead of you."

"I'm going to go soon," he says. I shake my head. I have no idea how to get to him.

"Anthony, what if I were to come up there,

come back? What if I were to show you what we have, why we think this guy did it? Will that buy me some time? Will you wait?"

He clears his throat and I feel like I have something to go on.

"Do you want to kill your father because he's a terrible person or do you want to kill him because he did something to your mother? Those are two very different things. What you're doing now is showing premeditation. You got a gun already right before you called me, right?"

"Yes." My heart sinks. I was bluffing, but he's not. I need to make this stop. What can I do? So far, he is listening to me. It has to be enough, right? I think to myself.

"If I come to see you, will you stop? I'm going to get on a flight tonight. Will you wait?"

"Yes."

"Do you want to kill your dad?"

"Look, I'm not a psychopath. I don't want to just kill someone for no reason, but he has to pay for what he did to my mom."

"If he didn't do it," I say. "If it were someone else—"

"I don't know." I can feel him shrug.

"You have all the time in the world to do this. Will you give me some time to show you what we have? To prove to you that there's a lot of doubt about whether your father is the one who did it."

"Yeah, sure. Only if you come tonight."

"Okay, I'm going to get the ticket right after I hang up from you, okay? Please don't do anything."

"I won't, but only if you come tonight."

He snaps and hangs up. I'm shaking partly from the cold, but mostly from the threats. I pace back and forth trying to decide what to do. Do I call the police, put him in protective custody, or do I wait it out and believe Anthony about what he said? I'm at a loss. One thing's for sure. Either way, I am getting a ticket to Seattle.

I make arrangements to fly out and find a flight that I can make five hours from now out of Ontario Airport, which is right down the hill from Big Bear. I talk to Violet over dessert. I try my best to explain what is about to happen. She listens carefully for a long time, and I look away from my phone, really wanting to make sure that she understands.

"I'm really sorry. I guess I could say it's outside of my control, but it's not. I could stay, of course, and just ignore his threats, but I'm worried. I'm worried he's going to do it. He's going to kill his father and his father might be the one who killed his mother."

"Can't you just tell the police that he's making these threats?"

"Yes, they could sequester him, but Anthony and I formed a relationship, a bond. I think what he wants is just to get to the truth. What if his father did do it? That's a possibility."

I had told her about the shaky alibi and went over the various details of the case.

"I feel like if I can go up there and I can talk to him, convince him to give the authorities more time, then nothing has to go to the police. His relationship with his father can possibly be salvaged. He won't be arrested, he won't be detained in any way, put on any psychiatric hold, nothing like that."

"What if you're wrong?" Violet asks.

She sits back in the chair and that's the one question that has been spinning around in my head for a long time.

"You've got a savior complex, you want to help everyone, but you can't always do that. You know that, right?" she asks.

"I have to try, Violet. I know you want me to stay here for the weekend. I know that it's a disappointment that I have to go again. Even if I make a lot of mistakes, there are other times when I follow my gut, it ends up being the right thing."

"What are you talking about?" She crosses her arms.

The goodwill of the day has disappeared and she's back to the pouty teenager that I remember so well from before.

"You know what I'm talking about. I didn't tell anyone when I came to look for you, it was a hunch. Everyone was giving up. I didn't even tell Luke."

"Then you found me," she says, "you're going to milk that for a while."

"No, I'm not going to milk it. There're just certain things that I have to do."

"I know you. I know you Kaitlyn," Violet says. "You believe certain things, and nothing will change your mind."

"Yes."

"But what if you're wrong?"

"I'll give you that. There's a good likelihood that I am wrong. Let me just say I'm sorry already for everything, but then there are things that I just have to do. I think I can stop him from making a terrible mistake. Even if his father did do it, if Anthony goes and makes good on his threat, it would be a mistake because it would ruin his life. He'll serve time. He'll never be the same. And vengeance is fiction. You can never really avenge anyone. You just take out your anger on someone else. Vengeance is not his to get. It's his mother's and she's dead. He can just get justice and learn to forgive and move on. I may be making a mistake,

I'll give you that, but I have to try. I have to go and I'm sorry, but I will be back, and we will do this again. I promise you that."

Chapter 34

I take the last flight available and land in a nearly empty SeaTac airport. With a rental car, I drive an hour to Olympia and meet up with Anthony at a McDonald's a biking distance away from his house.

"I hope you weren't waiting too long," I say after a brief embrace, in which he barely raises his arms to hug me back.

"I've been here for hours," he says. "I didn't think you would show."

"I promised I would."

He shrugs.

"Adults make all sorts of promises they never keep."

I know he's talking about his dad. I offer to buy him some dinner or a late-night snack, whatever he wants, and luckily, he takes me up on it.

"Three orders of French fries," he says. "I'm hungry."

"What about a burger?"

"No, I'm not eating meat anymore."

I'm about to tell him that the French fries are likely cooked in the same oil as the burgers, but I bite my tongue. He gets a milkshake as well. I opt for an order of fries with a Sprite and sit across from him in the brightly lit 24-hour fast food restaurant with uncomfortable plastic chairs and tired staff who fill their time snacking. The silence between us is deafening and the noise of the humming sounds of the kitchen reverberate in my head until I say something to make it stop.

"Look, Anthony, I'm here. I don't know how else to say it except that you promised not to hurt your dad and I want you to keep that promise."

"I made no such promise. I said I wouldn't do it tonight if you came."

"Well, I took a flight, rented a car to drive here using money that I don't have for this trip."

"You've done a lot more for me than any of the other cops here, but that doesn't change the fact that my dad killed her."

"No, he didn't. Or at least, I don't know that for sure and neither do you."

"He had an alibi, but he doesn't have one anymore."

"Anthony." I take a deep breath, popping a French fry in my mouth. "There's a lot about all of this that I know nothing about because I'm not privy to that information. The police can't reveal everything they have because otherwise, it's going to leak out and that will make it harder for them to make the case."

"Can you talk to them? Can you try to get more information? I won't tell anyone."

Suddenly, the mature, confident young man before me switches back to the child that he really is. The teenager who's no longer wise beyond his years but is a sad little boy who misses his mother.

"There's someone else that they have in mind. He's a serial killer who's responsible for a lot of murders in this area. They're putting the case together as we speak."

I fill him in about Jodie and the cabin, including as many details as I can, the ones that aren't going to repulse him or push him away. He listens carefully, nods, and I feel like I'm getting somewhere.

"Where is he now? Is he under arrest while they're making this case?"

"No, unfortunately, he's gone. They're looking for him. We were going to arrest him, but someone tipped him off."

"Are you going to try to find him?"

"The cops are doing their best."

"I'm tired of hearing that," Anthony says. "You know they're not."

"The FBI's working this case as well," I add. "I've met the agent in charge, and she's very competent. She was the one who found the evidence, who got his DNA to link up. She's very tenacious."

"So, she's a lot like you?" He smiles.

"Yes, you can trust her. Everyone is looking for him and his car."

"Don't you think he switched cars by now, maybe he has another identity?"

"Of course, but once he gets onto the FBI Ten Most Wanted, things will change."

"Yes, are you sure about that?" He sits back.

I wasn't, I wouldn't lie. I couldn't lie. I wasn't too sure of many things nowadays except that I have to stop this child from taking the law into his own hands, from killing his father, from ruining the rest of his life.

We talk for a little while about his mom, what he misses most about her and how life has been with him with his father and stepmom. His father is a first-grade ass; controlling and narcissistic. The type of person who always believes himself to be right and he takes no one else into consideration. After we finish our fries, I ask him point blank if I can trust him to go home and not do anything that I wouldn't approve of. He tilts his head and smiles a little.

"Only if I can go with you," he says, "tomorrow."

I had let it slip out that I was going to be staying with Donald Clark, the retired FBI agent who was instrumental in putting this whole case together linking up those bodies and making me believe that one man could have been responsible for all of their deaths.

Since this trip up was last minute and ridiculously expensive, I am living on credit cards now; ones I will have to pay off with a lot of overtime. I didn't want to pay for any more hotel rooms, and Donald was kind enough to offer me the guest room. The one mistake that I've made was opening up to Anthony that we had plans to go back to David's house tomorrow and talk to the neighbors again.

"You absolutely cannot come with us," I say. "It's out of the question. Besides, don't you have school?"

"I don't care about that. I want to come. I want to talk to Donald. I want to see if he believes that my mom was killed by this guy as much as you do."

"No, absolutely not," I say categorically and

tell him to go home and not do anything stupid. Early the following morning, however, my resolve falters and I pick him up, enabling his truancy. The three of us drive down to North Portland to visit David Trincia's house.

Chapter 35

I might be a sucker for letting Anthony come along, but I didn't fight too hard to make him stay. I know that he needs a resolution, he needs to believe in something. One day off from school is not going to be the end of the world.

Donald is in a happy, cheery mood; the way he had been ever since David Trincia had become the primary suspect. Even the fact that Trincia is now missing, and we cannot account for his whereabouts doesn't seem to faze him much, because he was right all along and now we all believe him.

Donald proves to be a nice buffer for me and Anthony, and they get so friendly that I wonder if I have become the buffer for the two of them. Anthony really takes to him, this older retired gentleman, asking him all about his work at the

FBI and his career highlights. He doesn't seem fazed at all by the dark and gruesome stories, but rejoices in the good moments when the missing are found and families are reunited.

"Have you ever thought about going into law enforcement?" Donald asks.

We grab lunch at a local coffee chain.

"I was going to do something with art later on, in college maybe."

"Well, we do have graphic artists working there, doing facial reconstruction, that kind of thing. If you're interested in any of this whatsoever, which it seems to me like you are, I'd encourage you. You got to get the four-year degree; major doesn't matter too much. Then you can apply to the academy, see if you have what it takes."

Suddenly, I smile at him, noting that his mood and perception about his career with the federal government has somehow changed, given the outcome of this case. When we had met before, he seemed really put upon, angry, frustrated. But now everything about the last forty years seems to be out in a different light.

"Look, I don't want to sugarcoat anything," Donald says, practically reading my mind. "You do get the ungrateful bosses; the terrible colleagues and you do have to learn how to work with them no matter what. Still, it might be a good fit for you."

"I'll think about it," Anthony says, changing everything about his demeanor. He sits up straight, broadens his shoulders, and stops twiddling his thumbs. For a second there I even think that his voice deepens.

He hasn't had many positive male influences in his life, especially father figures who believed that he could amount to something, I know that much. I wonder how much he would've connected with Steven; Cora's boyfriend, the man who seemed to be everything that she was looking for. Suddenly, I have a pang of regret and sadness for everything that this family wouldn't experience in the future; a lifetime of possibilities that they can never get back. Maybe Anthony can have a good life, despite all of that become someone that his mother would be proud of.

We finish lunch and head to David Trincia's address; the all too familiar street and house where I know we will not find him ever again. We talk to the neighbors, not pretending to be anyone that we are not. They mention that the police and the FBI had already talked to them, but they go over their stories trying to be as helpful as possible.

After a few short conversations, I know that we're not going to get anywhere, but I politely listen nevertheless, take notes just in case something comes up. It doesn't. Donald knocks on one last house, but I head toward Trincia's place to take one last look around. It had been scraped by the crime scene investigators, checked inside and out, every nook and cranny. What they found, I do not know, what else is there to get.

Absentmindedly, I flip open the mailbox attached to the wall next to the front door just to see if there's anything inside. There are a few letters, bill collectors likely, addressed to David, the usual advertisements for the local city council election, and then, right underneath, on the second to last envelope, I spot the name Rhys Hillier along with his address. Donald and Anthony step closer, and I wave it at them.

"You think it's somebody who lived here before?" I ask.

Donald hesitates.

"He's been in this house for years," he says.

I look at the envelope. It came from First Regional Bank.

We stare at the letter, the three of us huddled together, not at all suspicious. I suddenly realize we need to move away from his house. I look through the rest of the letters and this is the only one addressed to

Rhys Hillier. I grab the letter and lead the way back to the car. We are stealing mail after all, a federal crime. In the car, the three of us peer at the letter, looking at it, feeling it, wondering about the First Regional Bank that had sent it. I tell myself not to get my hopes up. It could be nothing after all.

"It could be a neighbor," I say. "Maybe they misprinted the address, or someone else who had lived at this house. I know I get old mail for a while whenever I move."

"Yes, whenever you move," Donald corrects me. "But you live in an apartment for how long? A year or two? He has been at that house for years. It's almost paid off."

"Do you think it's a friend of his?"

Donald shakes his head and gives me a wink.

"We have to open it."

I hate the fact that Anthony's here, but there's nothing I can do about it. We are already playing a role in him skipping school today. Adding to the truancy charge, we have obstruction of correspondence, a federal offense.

Here we are, knowing there's nowhere else for us to go from here except to open the envelope. I tear into it, ripping one piece along the sealed, glued portion up at a time, creating a little zigzag design on the back.

When I open the letter itself, my mouth drops.

It's a bank statement belonging to Rhys Hillier at David Trincia's address. The charges are from all over the Pacific Northwest. Two of them stand out, as one is from a Target and another from a nearby gas station in Olympia, Washington, on the day that Anthony's mother was abducted and murdered.

When I look up at Donald, our eyes meet, and I know exactly what he's thinking.

"This guy was there. This puts him in that location, right?"

I nod quietly.

"But only if he is in fact using the name Rhys Hillier," I say.

"Do you think he is?"

I shrug.

"We need more proof, more evidence."

I admit, "I don't know what else they took from that house, but now I wish that we hadn't opened this envelope. What if this is the only evidence that ties him to the scene of your mother's murder?" I say the words out loud and immediately regret them when I see the tears welling up in Anthony's eyes.

"No, that's not what's going on," Donald jumps to his rescue, "not at all. That's not what you meant, right, Kaitlyn?"

"No, not at all, no," I backtrack. "I'm sure they found more. This is just a crumb, one among many. We're going to get him, I promise."

Anthony nods, his upper lip quivering.

I let out a little sigh of relief, but then something else catches my attention. At the upper left-hand corner, the address that's attached to the bank statement is in Cannon Beach, Oregon, rather than the Portland address listed on the front of the envelope. I point the discrepancy out to Donald, who smiles at the corner of his lips.

"One must be a delivery address, and one must be the one he uses in Cannon Beach," he proposes.

I feel myself forming a little smile as well. "Could this be it? Could this be where he's hiding?"

"He wouldn't be stupid enough to go back there, would he"? Anthony suddenly says, shattering both of our hopes.

"Let's hope he is. But there're no guarantees, of course," I add. "We should probably give this to the FBI, the cops working the case."

"Yes, we could do that," Donald says, "or we could go there ourselves, check it out, take a little initiative."

I start to shake my head.

The three of us form quite a motley crew of private investigators. Yes, we have a lot of professional experience, but neither of us have jurisdiction here. We have already stolen his mail, and now we're going to show up at an address where he could possibly be hiding under a false name.

What if we find something there? What if we find another missing woman? What if we find a body? All that stuff is probably going to get kicked out of court.

"Inevitable discovery."

"You know that it all will depend on how good his lawyer is to prove that."

"I don't know any of that," Donald says.

"We have to give it a try."

"If we get the cops involved right now, I don't know how it's going to work out, and we don't even know what we're going to find. Let's just go there and let them know what we're doing. Let's ask for forgiveness rather than permission."

He tries to convince me further, but he doesn't have to. I'm already sold. I don't want to wait for warrants, red tape, or anything else for that matter. I want to find out if this is him before he has a chance to leave.

Chapter 36

The drive takes about three hours, but it's a scenic route, surrounded by dense forests that make me feel like I'm in a different world. The trees tower over us, creating a canopy that shades the winding road.

As we get closer to the beach, the forest starts to thin out, and we catch glimpses of the sparkling Pacific Ocean through the trees. Soon, we emerge from the forest onto the coastline, and I'm immediately struck by the sight of the enormous rock stacks rising up from the coastal waters. The waves crash against them, creating a mesmerizing rhythm that seems to reverberate throughout the landscape.

The most striking of these rock formations is Haystack Rock, which looms above us as we drive into the small, picturesque town of Cannon Beach. Population 1500.

It's overcast, but the rain has subsided for now. Seemingly all the town's residents have come out to Main Street to patronize its coffee shops, restaurants, walk their babies in strollers, and chase after toddlers in the local park.

On the drive, Donald and I reiterate to Anthony that we're not expecting to find anyone there. We have an address, but there are no guarantees that he will be there, that he is still using this name, that it's even him who this bank statement belongs to. Mostly, we say this to try to tamp down expectations, both Anthony's and ours. The trip here is a complete shot in the dark, and part of the way, I start to feel ridiculous that we're coming along at all.

We should have something better to do with our time, and we shouldn't be leading this impressionable teenager on a wild goose chase for a serial killer that law enforcement along the entire West Coast is looking for. Yet here we are doing this exact thing. Occasionally, I try to change the topic of conversation to something other than this case, but nothing seems to stick. Everyone's thoughts drift back to David Trincia, his whereabouts, and other possible identities he could have assumed.

After making one loop around town, I ask

where I should park, and Donald points to the first parking spot that he can find in front of a restaurant. Luckily, the traffic is light and the car that's behind me patiently waits as I make at least four turns back and forth before I get the car in just right parallel to the curb. The address listed on the bank statement is two blocks away. We decide to walk. The apartment is a second-floor walkup right in the alley behind Sleepy Monk Coffee Roasters. It seems like an illegal apartment to me, but also a good spot to hide out; a positive sign that David Trincia may, in fact, be here.

Not wanting to be too suspicious, I make my way down the alley first, taking my time to look around, pretending to be a tourist with my cell phone, but really taking pictures of the apartment, the alleyway, the door, and everything else.

Donald and Anthony anxiously wait for me to finish while inhaling the sweet scent of the fresh brewed coffee coming out of the local shop on the corner. When we meet up again, I show them the photographs as we try to formulate a game plan. Donald and I go back and forth about the pros and cons of knocking on the door, taking him by surprise, or simply waiting around here and trying to confront him on the street when he doesn't have as much opportunity to escape. Then Anthony adds that, in fact, he has the least opportunity to escape and run away when he's in his apartment given the fact that there's probably only one way in and one way out.

"The apartment itself could have weapons," I point out. "Ones that he'd be willing to use to make a clean getaway."

We continue to argue, not so much taking sides, but oscillating from one position to the next, finding the pros and cons in all. There is no perfect way to approach this, and for a moment, I consider calling the local authorities, knowing full well that they would tell us to back off until they arrive.

Then, out of the corner of my eye, I spot a man with sloped shoulders walking out of Rhys Hillier's apartment.

———

My heart jumps into my throat. My hands start to tremble. The focus in my eyes goes in and out as I try to figure out in a few seconds whether that is in fact David Trincia. He's got the familiar slouch to his shoulders even more pronounced now. He's wearing a baseball cap and his hair is longer than I remember. When I look a little closer, I see that it's a wig, and when he turns briefly in my direction, I know that it's him.

My eyes meet Donald's. He gives me a nod,

but a nod to do what? I don't have my weapon on me. We haven't called the authorities, so at most, this would be a citizen's arrest.

"Put your hands up. Police."

Donald is one step ahead. He extends his weapon pointing it at Trincia's back. Trincia flinches.

"Turn around slowly. Put your hands up," Donald instructs.

He has a smirk on his face, a little smile.

"This must be a mistake, sir," Trincia says.

"Put your hands up, Trincia."

"I'm not David Trincia," he slips, saying his first name.

His face tightens, realizing that he has said too much. Even if he hadn't, we know it's him.

"Put your hands up or I'll shoot," Donald says.

His grip on the gun, a Sig Sauer P229 9mm, is firm. He has his finger on the trigger, supporting it firmly with his left hand.

Trincia starts to move his hands as if he is about to lift them up but then reaches inside his jacket quicker than I would have thought possible for a man his age. A gun appears. Donald shoots, but Trincia's bullet grazes his left arm. His gun falls to the ground. I duck down to grab it. When I look up, Trincia is halfway down the block. All around us people are running, screaming. Some run over to Donald, others move out of the way. A child is crying. Trincia weaves in and out between the pedestrians, using them for cover and shelter.

Briefly, I look back at Donald and see Anthony cradling his head, hoping that he will be okay but not wanting to let Trincia get away. He disappears out in the distance, and I realize that he's gone behind one of the buildings. When I run around the corner, I see him holding on to his arm and note that he has been injured as well.

He seems to be making a wide circle. He runs around one corner and the next, probably trying to get back to his car. A few moments later, we are only a block away from the Sleepy Monk Coffee Roasters where Donald is still lying on the ground.

He heads toward his car. That's when I see an opening. I have to make him stop before this becomes a car chase. I stop myself from running, try to slow my breathing, and raise Donald's pistol. My eyes lock onto him and I squeeze the trigger.

His body goes rigid in mid stride as the bullet rips into his thigh. He falls to the ground, and the gun clatters across the pavement a few feet away. He struggles to reach for his weapon but I get there in time to kick it away. This part of the street has cleared out.

"You're under arrest," I say as he grabs his leg and winces in pain.

I'm about to read him his rights when

Anthony appears in my peripheral vision, holding the gun that I had kicked away, and points it at David's head.

"You killed my mother and now, you're going to die."

"Anthony, no," I say, reaching for the barrel and physically pushing him away.

"Get away from me, Kaitlyn. I'm not going to let this son of a bitch live."

"You want to find out the truth?"

My mind starts to race. How do I get him to stop?

It's not so much that I want to save this asshole's life but more that I want him to pay for what he did. I want him to take responsibility. I want him to be there in court to see all the victims and all the victims' families.

"If you want to know everything that happened to your mother, everything that he did, and you want him to pay for that by spending the rest of his life in prison, then you can't execute him right here. That's too good for him, Anthony. You know that."

Anthony's hand begins to shake. He swallows hard but then he makes the grip firmer.

"No," he says. "He's going to die. He's going to die either way. He's not going to get away with any of it."

"But if you kill him now, that's it. You don't get

to make him pay. You don't get to make him suffer even a little bit. If you shoot him now, that's too good for him."

I reach for the gun in his hand, and his grip loosens. He lets me take it from him. I let out a deep sigh of relief.

Somewhere in the distance, I hear sirens. The cavalry is coming. They'll be here soon. I put handcuffs on Trincia and take him away.

Trincia hears them, too, and makes one last-ditch effort to fight for his freedom. He kicks me in the leg. I buckle and drop to the ground. He tries to make a run for it but Anthony jumps on him and punches him in his face and the back of his head.

I should probably have pulled him off quicker, but I don't bother. I let him take some of his rage out on this man until there's blood all over his face and he struggles to breathe.

"Okay, Anthony, that's enough," I say quietly.

Tired and with his knuckles bloodied, there's a smile on Anthony's face. He has gotten what he wanted, the ability to inflict a little pain on the man who had taken so much from him.

Chapter 37

David Trincia was taken into custody by the Cannon Beach police and transported to Portland, where the case against him for the kidnapping of Jodie Schmidt was going to be taking place. Three murder cases are going to be tied to him in addition to the kidnapping, rape, and assault case of the woman who had survived and lived to tell the tale, but hers would go to court first and the others would be prosecuted in due time. Because the murders had occurred over a period of years in different jurisdictions, it would be hard to build the cases all at once.

Over the course of numerous interrogations and conversations with Detective Clint Patterson and Special Agent Jennifer Rivers, David Trincia had decided that it was in his best interest to come forward and eventually admit to being in the cabin and coercing his coworker, Celeste Griedier, into putting the deed to the cabin in her name.

He also admitted that she had no knowledge of anything that he was going to do there, but I would later learn that her husband didn't believe it. He was horrified by the fact that his wife was on friendly terms with one of the Northwest's most prolific serial killers. He filed for divorce a little before David Trincia's case went to trial.

When questioned about what exactly led him to killing these people, what prompted his attacks, he said that ever since he was a young boy, he had the feeling that an alien or some sort of other-worldly being had entered his body, and this alien or demon, he had used the words interchangeably, refused to leave until he gave him what he wanted. The calls to action were persistent, grew louder over the course of days and weeks until he couldn't keep them away any longer.

The first time these incessant thoughts had overpowered him was when he was still a teenager, and he'd killed his best friend by luring him into the woods behind their high school. The boy, Benny, was a popular track and field star who maintained his friendship with David even though he wasn't very much liked and was often bullied in school. He tried to make others care for him as much as he did because they were friends from childhood. Despite all this, David couldn't make the demons go away. He knew that he had to kill him.

When Jennifer Rivers checked on whether the story could possibly be true because no one had any inkling that anything like this had happened when he was in high school, she did indeed find that a close friend of his was found strangled in the woods behind his house. David was interviewed in the matter, but nothing had ever happened because no one in town suspected that a local person, let alone a teenager that everyone knew could have done something so horrible.

In addition to the confession, when Jennifer pressed him harder about any possible tokens or mementos that he had kept from his victims, he reluctantly revealed that in his bedroom, under the floorboards next to the dresser, they would find a box with little mementos from every one of his crime scenes. It was the fate that tied it all together. When he revealed this fact, I watched the way that a calmness came over him, his face relaxed, he sat back and seemed almost at peace like finally someone knew the truth besides him, and the burden would no longer be his to carry.

The box of his knickknacks was a treasure trove of evidence. That's where we found Cora's heart-shaped locket with the broken chain that Anthony had given her for Mother's Day among other things. It tied him to all the crime scenes that we had, additional ones that still needed to be investigated and victims who still needed to be identified. It also provided law enforcement with DNA evidence that tied him to those victims and DNA evidence that was missing from the crime scenes.

In addition, we also found evidence of his snooping on the preschool to which Luke and I had followed him. He had made notes about the children and the parents, clearly looking for his next victim. After we notified the school about his silver BMW and his license plate number, there were more notes about administrators coming to talk to him and asking him to leave.

Though the case was largely solved with more evidence than we could even imagine having, this was only just the beginning of David Trincia going through the legal process and the prosecution actually making a case and proving all of this in court to a jury that would eventually convict him. The journey ahead would be long and treacherous and, luckily, I would not need to be part of it.

What I was there for, however, was Anthony, to tell him that his father was indeed with his newest girlfriend, the one he was cheating on his stepmother with. It had been confirmed. The girlfriend had a husband and didn't want to come forward, but eventually did, and they were seen on tape eating dinner in a diner in a different county at the time when Anthony's mother was being killed by David Trincia. I promised Anthony that I would never tell a soul what he had wanted to do to his father, and he thanked me for stopping him.

"You have no idea how close I was to pointing a gun in his face or stabbing him through the heart. Any number of things that I had imagined doing, calling you was the last resort," he added. "I knew that you wouldn't come. It was a cry for help and then I could blame you for not being there for me but when you showed up, it changed everything."

It would still take a while for Anthony's relationship with his father to improve, for Anthony to forgive him and move on or perhaps just accept his father for who he was and love him nevertheless. The last bit would be the hardest, but I hoped that that would be possible despite his faults, because, with time, maybe they both could grow to understand each other. Not so much as father and son, but as adult men who love each other despite their differences. Perhaps that's just hopeful thinking on my part and that repairing that relationship was impossible, but I've seen a lot crazier things happen.

Before going back home to LA, I wish Captain Carville congratulations on his upcoming retirement and stop by Donald's house to say goodbye.

His wife, of course, treats me to pie and we catch up. There's a peacefulness to him now, a happiness that's difficult to describe. The anxiousness of the unsolved case seems to be gone.

I ask him, "What are you going to do with all of your extra time now? Take up fishing, golf?"

He smiles at me. "We have plans to travel."

"And then?" I ask.

"I'm thinking of working on a book about this case, about everything that has happened. Maybe you could share some notes with me, read it over when I have a draft?"

"Of course, I'd love that," I say.

"You're just not going to let this go, are you? You and I both know that this is just a beginning. We've got to make sure that it all goes to court, every single one of those murders is prosecuted."

"How many are they up to now?" I ask.

"He had mentioned thirteen different cases. Do you think he's lying about any, embellishing, trying to make himself the most important serial killer that ever lived?"

"I thought about that, but I'm not so sure. He never wrote to a newspaper; he never taunted the police with the fact that he was out there committing these crimes. I get the sense that he was really tormented by this demon, this alien. He seems to use the two words interchangeably, as you've noticed, and that makes me think that he is at peace now. That's probably why he confessed. That was my thinking."

"Exactly," I say. "For the thirteen cases, not all of them are bodies that we have. He's going to be pointing investigators in many different directions. It's going to be a lot of cases, and you're going to make yourself a part of that?"

"As long as Jennifer and Clint don't mind," he says, giving me a wink. "I like being helpful."

I exchange glances with his wife and we both laugh, knowing that him volunteering to help really means that he'll insert himself into any situation that he deems appropriate because, well, he knows the best way to solve the crime, doesn't he?

Donald asks me about Luke and our plans, and I tell him that we're going to get married and to expect an invitation.

"I like the sound of that."

⸻

Thank you for reading the Girl Hunted. Want to find out what happens when Kaitlyn investigates the brutal murder of a famous actress while getting ready to walk down the aisle? **1-click Girl Shadowed (Book 9) now!**

A beautiful young woman's mutilated body is found in the sand near the breaking waves of the

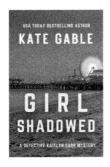

Pacific Ocean. When Detective Kaitlyn Carr is called to the scene, she discovers that it belongs to Emilia Cruz, an actress on a popular Netflix show, who had just attended the Screen Actors Guild Awards and is still wearing her gown from the night before.

As Kaitlyn begins her relentless pursuit of the truth, she uncovers a shocking secret: Emilia had recently joined a wellness cult led by an enigmatic figure who promises enlightenment through unconventional methods. The cult's obsession with green juices and extreme food restrictions raises suspicions, but Kaitlyn's investigation takes an unexpected turn when Emilia's old high school boyfriend, hailing all the way from Iowa, emerges as a potential suspect.

Caught between the chilling possibilities of a fanatical cult and the haunting presence of an obsessed ex-lover, Kaitlyn must navigate a treacherous path to expose the true culprit. With each step closer to the truth, she unravels a dark mystery that threatens to shatter the glitz and glamour of Hollywood.

Meanwhile, as Kaitlyn delves deeper into the investigation, she finds herself standing at the precipice. With her wedding to Luke Galvinson, an FBI agent, fast approaching, Kaitlyn must balance the demands of her personal life and her pursuit of Emilia's killer.

In this page-turning sequel, follow Detective Kaitlyn Carr as she tackles her most perilous case yet, unraveling a twisted tale of deception, obsession, and the high stakes of love and justice in the City of Angels.

1-click Girl Shadowed (Book 9) now!

Can't get enough of Kaitlyn Carr? Read the **Girl Hidden (FREE Novella)** now!

If you enjoyed this book, please don't forget to leave a review on Amazon and Goodreads! Reviews help me find new readers.

If you have any issues with anything in the book or find any typos, please email me at Kate@ kategable.com. Thank you so much for reading!

About Kate Gable

Kate Gable loves a good mystery that is full of suspense. She grew up devouring psychological thrillers and crime novels as well as movies, tv shows and true crime.

Her favorite stories are the ones that are centered on families with lots of secrets and lies as well as many twists and turns. Her novels have elements of psychological suspense, thriller, mystery and romance.

Kate Gable lives near Palm Springs, CA with her husband, son, a dog and a cat. She has spent more than twenty years in Southern California and finds inspiration from its cities, canyons, deserts, and small mountain towns.

She graduated from University of Southern California with a Bachelor's degree in Mathematics. After pursuing graduate studies in mathematics, she switched gears and got her MA in Creative Writing and English from Western New Mexico University and her PhD in Education from Old Dominion University.

Writing has always been her passion and

obsession. Kate is also a USA Today Bestselling author of romantic suspense under another pen name.

Write her here:

Kate@kategable.com

Check out her books here:

www.kategable.com

Sign up for my newsletter:

https://www.subscribepage.com/kategableviplist

Join my Facebook Group:

https://www.facebook.com/groups/
833851020557518

Bonus Points: Follow me on BookBub and Goodreads!

https://www.bookbub.com/authors/kate-gable

https://www.goodreads.com/author/show/
21534224.Kate_Gable

amazon.com/Kate-Gable/e/B095XFCLL7

facebook.com/KateGableAuthor

bookbub.com/authors/kate-gable

instagram.com/kategablebooks

tiktok.com/@kategablebooks

Also by Kate Gable

Detective Kaitlyn Carr Psychological Mystery series
Girl Missing (Book 1)
Girl Lost (Book 2)
Girl Found (Book 3)
Girl Taken (Book 4)
Girl Forgotten (Book 5)
Girl Deceived (Book 6)
Girl Hunted (Book 7)
Girl Shadowed (Book 8)

Girl Hidden (FREE Novella)

FBI Agent Alexis Forrest Series
Forest of Silence
Forest of Shadows
Forest of Secrets

Forest of Lies
Forest of Obsession
Forest of Regrets

Detective Charlotte Pierce Psychological
Mystery series
Last Breath
Nameless Girl
Missing Lives
Girl in the Lake

Lake of Lies (FREE Novella)

Printed in Great Britain
by Amazon

58500380R00179